PRAISE FOR VIVIAN AREND

"If you've never read a Vivian Arend book you are missing out on one of the best contemporary authors writing today."
~ *Book Reading Gals*

"I personally think A Soldier's Christmas Wish is best described as a treasure. Heartfelt and engaging, but most of all, so very romantic."
~Karen, Goodreads Reviewer

"This is a wonderful love story, and it was a magical Christmas story. It was great to celebrate the holiday with the residents of heart falls."
~ Book Addict Live

"This was a great little holiday, feel good read (that can be read anytime). I really enjoyed the characters."
~ *Lexee Toste, Amazon Reviewer*

"The sad, nostalgic and heart-warming gamut of emotions one feels makes this book a must read."
~ *LM, Goodreads Reviewer*

"5 stars for a Christmas story that certainly can be read again.
~ *Lovingbooks1, Bookbub Reviewer*

"Another masterpiece of love and passion Ms. Arend and all I have to say is THANK YOU!"
~Romance Witch Reviews

A SOLDIER'S CHRISTMAS WISH

HOLIDAYS IN HEART FALLS: BOOK 2

VIVIAN AREND

ALSO BY VIVIAN AREND

Holidays in Heart Falls

A Firefighter's Christmas Gift

A Soldier's Christmas Wish

A Hero's Christmas Hope

A Cowboy's Christmas List

A Rancher's Christmas Kiss

The Stones of Heart Falls

A Rancher's Heart

A Rancher's Song

A Rancher's Bride

A Rancher's Love

A Rancher's Vow

The Colemans of Heart Falls

The Cowgirl's Forever Love

The Cowgirl's Secret Love

The Cowgirl's Chosen Love

~

A full list of Vivian's print titles is available on her website

www.vivianarend.com

A Soldier's Christmas Wish
Copyright © 2019 by Arend Publishing Inc.
ISBN: 978-1-989507-14-8
Edited by Anne Scott
Cover Design © Damonza
Proofed by Angie Ramey & Linda Levy & Manuela Velasco

www.vivianarend.com

1

"**W**ell, shoot."

Brooke Silver poked her head out of the small galley kitchen in time to see her father make a face. "What's wrong?"

He lifted a hand in the air, one finger pushed through a hole in his knitted slipper. "I blew a gasket."

A snort escaped her. "I hope your slipper was softer than the average gasket. Want me to grab you another pair?"

Her dad rose to his feet and waved off the suggestion. "I'll take care of it. You're making supper. I don't want to change jobs, because as limited as your cooking skills are, you're better than me."

There wasn't much she could say in argument to that. She went back to the simple meal she was making only to be distracted again by soft cursing from beside the front door.

"Having a tough day, Dad?"

No answer. Just the sound of something thumping against the floor then her dad shuffling out of the living room toward his room at the back of their small apartment.

She shrugged and focused on not burning the potatoes and eggs.

Their apartment, tucked into the upper corner of the garage, was small but efficient. The common kitchen and living space were in the middle, with a bedroom and private bathroom on either side. Her dad had built the addition himself before they'd moved out of the house in Heart Falls that they'd shared with Gram and Grandpa during her growing-up years.

While it wasn't the most luxurious of accommodations, and it definitely lacked in privacy, the price was right. Small-town mechanics did okay, but it was smart to keep expenses as low as possible. Sharing a living space with her dad wasn't a terrible thing, and they got along fine.

Yet there were times she wished for a little more space, and as her phone went off in her back pocket, Brooke let the grin come.

One reason she wouldn't mind a little more privacy—her boyfriend, Mack.

She held her phone against her shoulder while she gave the potatoes a quick flip. "Hey, cap. What's up?"

"Right now, nothing. It's quiet at the station, and I'm the only one on the schedule for the night." His voice was a deep rumble that soothed even as it lit a tingle inside her. "Want to come by later?"

She checked her watch. "Dad and I will be done with supper in about hour. You need me to bring anything over?"

"Just you." Low and husky. Definitely something on his mind.

After nearly a year of spending time together, Brooke could not only guess what that particular thing was, she was one hundred percent on board.

"See you soon," She hung up then slid her phone away so

she could serve dinner and drop the plates on the table. "Dad. Supper's ready."

He joined her, and they dug into the simple meal. While they ate, Gary Silver went over a few projects on the to-do list for the next couple of days, but Brooke could see something was off.

She examined him. "You're distracted. Something wrong?"

Her dad wrinkled his nose then leaned back with a sigh, folding his arms across his chest like a disgruntled two-year-old. "There's no more slippers."

Brooke had to repeat that one mentally, and she still wasn't quite sure what it meant. "No more slippers…where?"

Gary sighed again. "The ones your Gram made."

Ahh. It made sense now. "The multicoloured slip-ons she knit every night in front of the TV?"

"Yep. I put them all in a box. Every time one got a hole, I'd throw it out and grab a new one." He wiggled uncomfortably in his chair, face downcast. "I hit the bottom of the box. There's none left."

A jagged slice of pain struck her. Grandpa had been gone for a couple of years already, Gram a couple before that, but they'd been such a part of her life for so long it seemed impossible they weren't somewhere just around the corner.

Brooke laid her hand on her dad's forearm. "I'm sorry. I miss them too."

He nodded briskly, then looked as if he were about to change the topic back to engine repair and the block heater on the McMasters' van that seemed to be on the fritz at least once a month.

Something sad yet thoughtful drifted over his expression.

"Hard to believe we've hit December already, yet here we are heading into the holiday season. Doesn't feel right." Gary shook his head. "Silly that having gone through the last of the slippers is enough to knock me for a loop, but it's there."

"It's not silly to think about things we miss."

He pushed up from the table, grabbing the plates. "No use in dwelling on what we can't have. When it's gone, it's gone, and we shouldn't sit around moping. I suppose I'm wishing for that old-fashioned Christmas feeling, but there's not a lot we can do to make that happen."

The words hit her like snowballs in a surprise attack.

An old-fashioned Christmas?

She'd never heard him utter that sentiment before in his life. Gary Silver was pragmatic to the core. He wasn't staid or boring, but the man worked with nuts and bolts and believed everything had a place.

Her dad stepped around her, depositing the plates in the sink before twisting back to offer what was clearly a forced grin. "Thanks for cooking. I'll clean up. I suppose you're headed to see that guy."

Brooke stuck out her tongue at the running joke between them. "You pretending he doesn't have a name doesn't change anything. Mack is a very nice man, and yes, I'm going to see him."

Her father ignored her comment about Mack, instead raising a finger and pointing at her face. "You remember what your grandma said about silly faces. Next thing we know the wind will change, and you'll be stuck like that forever."

She snickered then slipped in to give him a hug before heading to her room for a quick wash up and to change into something a little nicer.

Spending time with Mack had been wonderful. He'd been a Canadian Air Force firefighter for a number of years. Now retired from active duty, he worked in the firefighting and emergency services industry as a civilian.

The big man was easy to talk with, definitely easy on the eyes, and everything about him fit her just right. They'd had surprisingly few squabbles considering how bullheaded she could be and the fact he was equally stubborn.

Nope, they pretty much got along like a house on fire—and the thought made her grin. Her firefighter cringed every time she used a flame-reference joke.

Their biggest issue had been finding places to be alone. Her living arrangement with her dad, and Mack's full-time residence at the fire hall meant someone, parental or volunteer, tended to show up at inconvenient times. Between stolen moments and a few spectacular getaways at hotels, though, they'd had enough opportunities to prove they fit just right in the physical department as well.

Was she ready for more? On one level—yes. Getting to say good night and not have to leave his arms would be an awesome change. Moving their relationship into more intimate territory and someday having family was something she hoped for.

But Brooke was pragmatic enough herself to figure if this relationship was right, eventually the next thing would happen. Neither of them had enough saved up to change their living circumstances. Mack got free accommodation at the station, but he'd been sending money to his parents and paying off debts. She'd just made the final repayment on her student loans.

Pushing to see if he wanted to move in together when they weren't able to afford a place would have been frustrating. And she wasn't going to ask him to move in with her when Dad lived down the hall.

Just...nope. Nope, nope, hell no.

Maybe in the new year she'd broach the subject. For now, while patience might be one of her superpowers, waiting sucked.

After slipping on a clean long-sleeved T-shirt in powder blue—Mack's favourite colour—she took the stairs down to the main level of the garage. She hauled open the oversized door so she could back her truck into the snowy winter night.

Holiday lights twinkled on the lampposts down Main Street as she made her way across town.

The fire hall parking lot held more cars than expected. Heart Falls was a small enough community that they only had one full-time firefighter—Mack—and the rest were volunteers. Brad Ford, the fire chief for the surrounding districts, also lived in Heart Falls, and as she made her way upstairs to the room above where the emergency vehicles were stored, she was surprised to discover not only firefighters, but Brad's wife, Hanna, as well.

A kitchen ran along one side wall, and in the corner, a gleaming fire pole allowed for quick-access slides to the ground level. In the center of the room rested a table large enough for more than a dozen people to gather. It wasn't full, but the place was far from empty.

Mack gave her a sheepish grin as she routed herself to the empty chair between him and Hanna.

He leaned in close, squeezing Brooke's fingers. "Sorry about this. I had no idea the guys were coming over tonight."

Across the table, Ryan Zhao offered a greeting, his jet-black hair swaying with the motion. His expression was polite as always, but a hint of amusement shone in his dark eyes. "Good to see you again, Brooke. You should just give up and become part of the volunteer firefighter team."

At Ryan's side, a wiry cowboy by the name of Alex approved the suggestion. "You seem to be here every time we are. Joining the team makes sense. It would make it so much easier for you to appreciate my company."

Mack pretended to stretch, then tossed a coaster off the table directly at Alex's face. "She's not coming to see you."

"That's what you think." Alex waggled his brows.

Masculine laughter rolled as the men responded to the

teasing, but before Brooke could offer a comeback, her friend Hanna caught her by the sleeve and tugged her from the table.

The teeny brunette spoke softly but with amusement as well. "Since you boys need official meeting time, we'll get out of your way." She grabbed a bag off the counter and held it enticingly toward Brooke. "I brought refreshments."

Mack looked slightly put out, but there really was no sense in sitting at his side while he talked shop with Brad, Alex, and Ryan.

Besides, the scent rising from the bag promised fresh gingersnaps. She might not be the best of cooks, but she was a top-notch cookie consumer.

Brooke patted Mack's shoulder in mock sympathy. "Don't worry. We won't eat *too* many of the cookies before you're done."

She dodged his teasing fingers then followed Hanna from the dining hall into the back living space where there was a separate, more comfortable room made specifically for quiet escape. Doors led off the room to the bunkhouse and shower rooms.

Hanna settled into one of the easy chairs, turning her soft smile in Brooke's direction. "I missed you at the last girls' night out. How has everything been going? Do you have big plans for Christmas?"

That was a stumper of a question, because until an hour earlier, Brooke hadn't. She pretty much had planned on following the same simple holiday agenda she and her dad had shared in the past, with Mack included, of course. Now she wasn't so sure.

An old-fashioned Christmas? What on earth did that mean?

She wanted to think about it a little more on her own first, though, so Brooke held her tongue and kept her puzzled thoughts to herself. Besides, she had a feeling her friend, with her glowing cheeks, had some news of her own to share.

"Still working on the details," Brooke offered simply before leaning forward and looking Hanna in the eye so she couldn't wiggle out of spilling the beans. "What's the special thing that's got you shining like a vintage chrome fender flare?"

Hanna didn't bother to pretend. "Oh, nothing too big and fancy. Just a nice family celebration with Brad, his dad, and his brother. Although we're trying to decide if we should pick Christmas Eve or the next morning to tell Crissy she's going to be a big sister."

Brooke had been right. She rose to her feet to offer an impulsive hug, one that Hanna returned enthusiastically. "That's so exciting. You and Brad must be thrilled."

They settled back into their chairs, Hanna's expression one of radiant joy. "We are. We decided there wasn't any use in waiting to have a baby. Not since Crissy's going on nine and eager to be a helper."

"When are you due?"

"June," Hanna said, stars shining in her eyes.

They chatted for a little longer, munching on warm gingersnaps, until the sound of chairs being pushed back and scraped along the floor echoed from the other room. The next minute, the door beside them opened and Brad marched in, Mack hard on his heels.

"Sorry for interrupting your evening," Brad offered as he made his way to Hanna's side. He knelt beside her chair and caught her fingers in his, kissing her knuckles while he stared at her with adoration. "Thanks for waiting for me."

"Always."

"Congratulations," Brooke offered. "I heard the news."

Brad's proud grin stretched from ear to ear, but it was the way he carefully curled his arm around Hanna as she stood by his side that proclaimed even louder how much he cared about his wife.

Brooke made plans to get together with Hanna later in the week, then Hanna and Brad headed home, leaving Brooke and Mack standing in the dining area.

Muffled noises continued to rise from the station hall below them. Brooke had been around often enough to recognize the sounds. "Someone working on the gear?"

"Alex and Ryan are packing emergency bags down in the hall. At least they're not in the room with us." Mack caught her hand and pulled her toward him. "Please tell me you can stay for a while."

Both of them had agreed there was no getting down and dirty while anyone else was in the station. As sad as that was, Brooke had something else equally important on her mind. She definitely needed to bend Mack's ear and pump him for ideas.

Plus, although sex was off the table, there was nothing to say they couldn't indulge in a bit of kissing during their brainstorming session.

~

It wasn't at all what Mack had in mind when he'd called her earlier. He tugged Brooke back into the living room, settled on the couch, and pulled her into his lap.

The way she curled up against him spoke of months of familiarity, and the hole inside him that ached to be filled chimed loud and clear.

Mack had plans. Big, huge, life-changing plans. He'd been thinking about this seriously ever since the summer. Spending time with Brooke was one of the rightest things in his world and he had no intention of missing out on something so spectacularly perfect.

Only, there was one thing he hadn't yet figured out. Possibly two. But as he curled his hand around the back of her neck and tugged their lips together for a slow lingering kiss, Mack dreamed about the ring he'd purchased a month ago and how much he wanted to slip it on her finger.

Everything about their relationship had been so comfortable from the start that he wanted this one event to be different. Not different as in awkward, but he wanted the moment he proposed to be big and memorable so they could look back on it and smile. An epic event to share down the road with friends and a family.

Which was the first reason why the box filled with the shiny ring was still tucked away safely beside his bed. The second reason?

Brooke's father...

Mack pushed aside his concerns and focused on the woman cuddling close on his lap, stroking her fingers down his arms at a slow and steady pace that heated him up, nevertheless.

He nipped at her lower lip and she laughed, running her hands up to tangle her fingers in his hair.

She caught hold and tugged lightly. "Hey. I need some advice," she said.

Brooke wiggled off his lap, but he adjusted her position so that her legs remained draped over his, needing that connection even as he lifted his gaze to meet her eyes. "You should definitely buy a new set of lingerie. I like your blue set," he told her.

Her mouth fell open for a second before she rolled her eyes. "Not that you get much chance to see me in my underwear," she teased. "It seems every time we get alone, we're both in too big of a hurry to get naked to worry about any kind of fashion show."

Her off-the-cuff comment caught him off guard, but he filed it away to think on more thoroughly later as he gave her his complete attention. "What's the real question?"

"My dad was making noises about wanting an old-fashioned Christmas, and I'm not quite sure what he was talking about." She stared at the ceiling. "But I don't want to ask him straight out because what triggered this was discovering the last pair of slippers my grandma knit is gone. So...is he wishing for some of the stuff that used to happen when she was around? I'm not sure what old-fashioned means, but if I can guess, that will make the holiday more meaningful than him giving me some kind of list and me checking things off."

Wow. This could be an interesting challenge.

Mack sat up straighter, his brain already looping through possible ideas. "I don't know a ton about typical Christmas traditions—I didn't have a hell of a lot myself growing up, being in a military family and moving all the time, but that sounds like something I would love to help you with."

As well as being a chance to make memories of their own. A chance to maybe figure out the perfect time to seal their lives together?

Possibly a chance to impress Brooke's father—

Not that Mack had any plans of asking the man's *permission* to marry her, but having Gary's approval and blessing would be a good thing. Right now it felt as if every time her dad caught a glimpse of Mack, his expression grew uneasy.

It was eerie, and frankly, it was annoying. Mack was a likable guy, dammit. Still, Gary managed to make him feel as if he were ten years old and caught with his hand in the cookie jar.

Brooke was already in motion. She pulled out a notebook and resettled at his side, opening to a new page and neatly titling the top *Old-Fashioned Christmas Plans*.

"I remember some of the things that Gram and Grandpa used to do during the holidays. I'm not sure why we stopped doing them. I guess when it switched to being just Dad and me, it became too much. It didn't feel necessary to celebrate the same way. But there were these cookies that he absolutely loved. I can't remember what they're called, but making a big batch of those would be one thing we could do." She wrinkled her nose. "If I can find the recipe."

Mack rocked an elbow gently into her side. "That would be one task I can definitely help you with considering your talents in the kitchen."

She gave him a raised brow. "I've heard rumours you've burnt a few meals here in the fire hall."

"Only when you distract me," he admitted as he stole a kiss. "Give me the notebook. You reminisce. What else do you remember?"

She handed over the book, her gaze sliding to faraway and long ago. She started slowly then spoke with more animation as the memories flooded in. Music, meals. All the things that had been a part of her world while growing up with Gary and her grandparents.

Brooke shook herself alert at one point and met Mack's gaze, a soft smile on her lips. "You would have liked my grandparents. They helped raise me, and yet it never really felt as if they were trying to fill in for my nonexistent mom. Dad was Dad, Gram and Grandpa were who they were, and we all got along. It was pretty sweet." Brooke was staring into space again. "It didn't seem special, but looking back, it really was."

Mack's gaze lingered on her as he considered his own growing-up years. "As kids, we don't realize what makes a memory. I remember going out to eat on Christmas Day. Depending where Mom was stationed, there was always a restaurant open, usually Chinese, and that was the simplest way to celebrate when Dad was in charge." Brooke's eyes widened and Mack laughed at her expression of near horror. "Don't look at me like that. Chinese food for Christmas was awesome because it was...a tradition. And while Dad cooked basic meals just fine, something other than meat and potatoes was a treat."

Brooke eased away, but she was nodding slowly. "Exactly. *Our* traditions... The old-fashioned Christmas Dad's looking for isn't about turn-of-the-century meals or candles on the tree."

He shuddered. It was impossible not to as an image of a firetrap rushed to mind.

Laughter escaped her.

Brat. He offered Brooke a glare. "You did that on purpose."

A gentle wink confirmed it before she went on. "We should focus on what we did have—the traditions we've skipped over the past few years. Those are *our* old-fashioned ways to celebrate." She frowned, concentrating. "I wonder if we have some pictures I could go through, because I swear we had decorations to put on the roof, but I can't picture them very well."

"Decorations, food—including the mysterious nameless cookies of unknown ingredients. And music, but you don't remember the exact song. This sounds simple," Mack teased.

Brooke tapped her fingers against his lips. "You were there last year for Christmas, and you *know* we kept it simple. This is your chance to help me up my game. Are you willing to take on the challenge?"

"It's exactly the kind of mission I want to take on," Mack assured her. "We'll have to work around my shifts here and yours at the garage, but if you can dig up a photo album or two, we can start making specific plans."

Which meant *he'd* be able to make specific plans—ones concerning forever. Because somewhere in the middle of making wonderful memories there was going to be a moment that would be just right, and he would be ready.

Before Christmas was over, he was determined to complete his mission: create the perfect memory of Brooke Silver accepting him as hers.

2

Brooke shrugged out of her winter parka, the warmth of the Buns and Roses coffee shop wrapping around her like a warm hug.

She'd barely placed her tote bag on the small tabletop when two strong arms trapped her and squeezed her tight.

"You've been a stranger," Tansy Fields complained when she finally let Brooke out of her grasp. The usually smiling blonde shook a finger in Brooke's face as if ready to put her name on Santa's naughty list. "But you're here now, so I forgive you. As long as you tell me you're going to make it to our next girls' night out."

Brooke settled in her chair, smiling at her friend. "Yes, I'll be there."

"Good, because we're losing most of our gal pals to some big shindig for the Stone and Coleman clans. Right now, as far as I know, it's just going to be you, me, Rose, and Hanna for the night."

Someone hit the bell for service up at the front counter and Tansy moved quickly to answer the summons.

Brooke let her go, knowing that as soon as there was a chance, Tansy would sneak out for another visit.

In the meantime, she had only a few minutes to get set up before Mack had promised to join her. Since neither of them had a long break, she might as well make their time together as efficient as possible.

She'd been digging for the last couple of nights, shocked to discover how little they had left from the days when she and her dad had lived with his parents. But then again, it had been fifteen years since her grandparents had moved into a seniors lodge and she and her dad had shifted locations to the apartment over the mechanical shop.

There hadn't been a lot of storage room, but the lack of knickknacks and mementos probably had more to do with the fact that fourteen-year-old Brooke had been in charge of packing up those items to keep or give to charity. Her father had been focused on keeping their livelihood going while settling his parents as best he could. Gram had just had a stroke, and Grandpa was completely focused on being there for her while they adjusted to their new surroundings.

Teenage Brooke had no idea what should be saved to help in memory-making and was now regretting her abysmal choices.

She had just opened the best photo album of the lot when Mack blasted into the coffee shop, cold air and wind sweeping in with him before he got the door shut.

He grinned across the room. "Jack Frost at your service."

Tansy shook her head in amusement from where she was working the espresso machine. "You turn my hot drinks into slushies, and I will find a way to get revenge."

"How about two large lattes and whatever the baking special is instead?"

"That would be cinnamon rolls with cream cheese icing.

Deal." Tansy turned her attention back to the order in front of her.

Mack dropped into the chair next to Brooke, leaning over to offer a quick kiss. "Hey."

The scent of him lingered—winter sharpness and the faintest layer of wood ash, because it seemed firefighters never completely got rid of the smoke that was part and parcel of their livelihood.

Brooke smiled warmly, laying her fingers on top of where he'd rested his hand on her thigh. "How long have you got?"

"Until noon or until my phone goes off with a summons for an emergency. How about you?"

"Noon as well. You want to see what I found?"

Mack adjusted his chair, sliding in so he could reach around her and nestle her close. It was an easy move, familiar and right, and the tension inside Brooke eased off enough that the next breath she took was deep and calming.

He was so comfortable to be around. And right now, that comfort helped ease the knot of worry she'd discovered tangled inside. It wasn't as if her dad would be super disappointed if things didn't work out. Her dad was accepting and pretty laid-back, so her unease wasn't about him.

Brooke took another deep breath and let it out slowly, leaning into Mack's side. "I don't know why I'm fixated on this. I mean, I know I always drill down on the details for anything I do, but it feels as if this is extra important. It doesn't make sense."

Mack tightened the arm wrapped around her, chuckling softly. The motion of his body rocked her. "You don't have to understand it to deal with it. Come on. Show me what you found, and we'll see if we can make some definite plans. If you can have a checklist to start working on, that will to help you relax a little."

Which was true, and far too revealing. "I should be worried

that you know all my idiosyncrasies and flaws," she muttered as she flipped to the start of the photo album.

Lips pressed to her cheek before he murmured softly in her ear, privately, just for her. "I like knowing all your secrets."

"I bet you do."

His hum of pleasure rumbled past her like a caress. "If you don't want me making public that I know where your ticklish spots are, you'd better share details so we can get this mission planned."

That made her laugh. Brooke twisted in her seat, offering an amused smile. "And the soldier pops out of hiding. I like it when he shows up."

"It's not as if he's on active duty anymore," Mack teased, and then he stole the photo album from under her hands. "The captain is currently taking charge since the civilian seems incapable of following orders."

Brooke laughed, then flipped through the pages, pointing to pictures and explaining who and what they were looking at as the memories flowed.

It wasn't the best of photo albums. Gram had obviously never heard of the scrapbooking craze, and Brooke hadn't been interested back in the day. It's entirely possible it had been Grandpa or her dad who had shoved these pictures into the magnetic album with disregard for chronological order.

"There's the house I grew up in. It's over on Elm Street, although they've done a bunch of renovations and added a second story."

Mack leaned in closer, then dragged a finger over the gaudy display of lights covering nearly every inch of the roof. "Someone had fun with lights and ladders. Lots and lots of fun..."

Tansy arrived with their drink order in time to hear his comment and she all but hooted with laughter. "Legend is, the Silver family started the tradition of Candy Cane Lane here in

Heart Falls. Everybody around them figured they were going to be blinded by lights anyway, so they may as well join in and put up Christmas decorations as well."

Tansy placed the drinks on the table along with cinnamon buns the size of Brooke's outstretched hand, then answered another summons.

Mack's amusement seemed to fade as he turned to Brooke. "But I was at your place last year, and you had no decorations up. Maybe one string of lights around the window in the shop."

She had to shrug. "It wasn't high on the priority list, I guess. I'm not sure. Maybe Grandpa was the one who instigated the house decorating, not Dad."

Mack nodded thoughtfully, leaning in to examine the house one more time before pointing to her notebook and demanding she write down a list of items. "Let's see if we can find what happened to the old decorations, but if we can't, I'll get creative."

"If you do find the old decorations, you have to update them because your electric bill would be fifty million dollars." The comment came from a new person joining them at the table. Rose Fields, Tansy's sister and the owner of the knickknack flower shop adjoining the coffee shop.

She smiled at Brooke before tilting her head at Mack, her long, dark brown hair sliding over her shoulders as she gave him a pointed look. "In case you want to be prepared, I should mention I'm having a sale right now on LED lights."

He grinned. "Brooke, add that to the to-do list. Decoration shopping at Rose's."

The guys at the next table called Mack's name, and he slid to his feet with an apology, joining the discussion about bonfire permits.

Rose took advantage of the opportunity to lean forward conspiratorially. "So, how goes it with you and Captain Hottie?"

Brooke shrugged. "Good. We're making some Christmas plans."

A look of growing excitement spread over her friend's face. "Are they big plans? Are they *shiny* plans?"

"I suppose. My dad made some comment about an old-fashioned Christmas, so we're trying to figure out what we did back when my Grandpa and Gram were still alive."

Rose all but wrinkled her nose in disgust. "You're killing my holiday hopes, lady."

A chuckle escaped before Brooke could stop it. "Because setting up an old-fashioned holiday isn't going to involve enough shopping at your store?"

Her friend pulled back slightly, all lightheartedness vanishing from her expression as she turned far more thoughtful. "You're serious. You're knee-deep in planning something that involves...your dad."

"Did I miss some memo saying there's supposed to be more on the agenda?"

"Oh my God. You're so clueless sometimes. For a smart person, that is." Rose glanced over to make sure Mack was still busy with the guys before she lowered her voice far enough that Brooke could barely make out the words. "You guys have been dating for a long time."

Okay, it was clear exactly where this was going and what dirt Rose was digging for.

While Brooke was willing to wait for the future to arrive—the one that included her and Mack in a full-time, full-on relationship—she wasn't willing to discuss her reasons for waiting ad nauseam with her friends.

Which meant bluffing. Bluffing was fine—better than fine, because pretending to be clueless was also amusing, and if she couldn't have Mack 24/7, then she'd take the entertainment factor of playing dumb.

"Nope. I'm still lost," she offered cheerfully.

Mack returned to the table as Rose shot to her feet to answer the bell from the far side of the shop.

Rose wiggled her fingers as she left, tossing one final comment over her shoulder. "At some point I'll toss you a map."

It was nearly impossible to keep a straight face. Brooke bit her bottom lip and offered her boyfriend what had to be a twisted smile, amusement bubbling inside.

~

Utterly aware of the time ticking past, but curious what had put that expression on Brooke's face, Mack settled into his seat then eyed her closer. She didn't seem to be upset, though, just fidgety. "What was Rose talking about maps for?"

Brooke shimmied her shoulders in a movement reminiscent of someone with snow melting down their back. "She might need another coffee or two. Nothing to worry about."

"Busy season for her. She's probably tired," he pointed out. He reached for the photo album and pushed the notebook back in front of Brooke. "Let's get back to work. We're going to track down decorations and adjust them if necessary. Did you find any recipes?"

"Oh, I did." She eagerly flipped to a different section of the book and showed him a half dozen recipe cards that had been stuck alongside totally unrelated pictures.

One quick glance was enough to show there was still a problem. "Any idea what language those are written in?"

"Should be Swedish."

Mack grinned. "And do you read Swedish?"

She shook her head but obviously had this part figured out. "There were a bunch of people who did at the seniors lodge where Gram and Grandpa lived. I figured I'd head there sometime and see if I can get a translation. I'm not sure which one of these is for the cookies, but it might be nice to have all the rest as well."

"More things to burn. Sounds about right." He swayed out of reach when she pretended to punch him. "You find anything else?"

"Mention of the song. Or the songbook it might come from. I swear it had the word *yule* in the title, but nothing came up when I googled it. I thought I might be able to ask around for help with that at the seniors lodge as well."

It wasn't your typical date destination, but over the years, Mack had spent a lot of time going to different places to meet with people. The Heart Falls Seniors Lodge was full of good, solid community members, and most of them loved to reminisce. "I'd like to come with you, but it'll have to be tomorrow afternoon."

"I can do that." Brooke flipped to another page in the book and held it up triumphantly. "This I do remember, and we don't need anybody to translate for us."

He eyed the page. A motley collection of items was pictured. Everything from a misshapen sweater to a teddy bear with one leg longer than another and mismatched eyes. "You're related to Tim Burton?"

A snort of laughter escaped her. "I don't remember when it started, but even though I got presents from the store for my birthday and throughout the year, Christmas presents were always handmade."

Another glance at the page and Mack saw wooden carved toys, knitted items. Paintings and other artistic endeavors. "Okay."

Brooke was staring at the page now, a soft glow in her expression. "This is the one tradition Dad and I kind of kept up with. I don't know that it's ever been *said* that we don't buy things for each other, but I usually make him a food basket—and no smart-ass comments about me burning things. He makes something in the shop or does something as simple as shining up my tools so I can start the new year with them good as new."

A sweet, happy sensation slid in. "Then I guess I didn't screw up too bad last year when I brought you that care package."

"Hey. You're right." She leaned on her elbows, photo albums forgotten, all happiness and light, with her long hair sliding over her shoulders. "Definitely putting that on the list."

"Care packages?"

"Homemade gifts," she corrected. "I'm not going to tell you what I'm making you, but if you're interested in giving me anything, that's now officially the rule."

Mack thought about the ring box now wearing a hole in his pocket. "So...just checking. Homemade is *just* for Christmas presents?"

She nodded decisively then dropped her eyelids to half-mast. "Because sexy lingerie is beyond both of our sewing abilities."

He laughed loud enough to catch Tansy's attention behind the counter. He pulled Brooke toward him and spoke softly. "That was wrong on so many levels. Number one, you have no idea what my sewing abilities are, and number two, dear God, I don't know why you'd be sewing anything like that for *me*."

She slipped her arms around his neck and gave him a quick kiss. A display of affection appropriate for a public place but hot enough to set a fire burning inside him.

Plus, he carried the warm glow in his heart out of the coffee shop and into the snowy December day.

3

Brooke put her tools away after the final tune-up of the day, cleaning her hands on a rag as she marched to where her father was poking around under his classic cruiser.

She bent over to make sure she wasn't about to startle him, and when he met her gaze, she offered a wink. "I'm done with the job on the Grahams' Chevy. I'm going to wash up quick then head out if you don't have anything you need me to do."

Her dad went thoughtful for a moment then shook his head. "I can tell it's the slow season. Barely Friday afternoon and we're already done? Don't go overboard with Christmas presents—we're going to have to keep the expenses down until we can convince everybody it's time for a tune-up for the new year."

"We have enough steady customers. We'll be fine," Brooke reassured him. She deliberately ignored his comment about the Christmas presents because she didn't want him even thinking about what might be happening.

She was still figuring out what she wanted to do for her homemade contribution to the celebration. This afternoon was about finding out more details. She and Mack had made an appointment to stop in at the home where Grandpa and Gram had lived until a few years ago.

"You'll be home for supper?" her dad asked.

"Maybe? I'm not sure what time Mack and I will be done. I don't know if he has any other plans. I might end up bringing him home with me."

Her father made a noise, but he was rolling back underneath the chassis and it was impossible to see his face.

The entire trip over to the lodge she worried at the idea that had been nagging her. It wasn't as if her dad had ever come out and said he didn't like Mack, but there were an awful lot of negative-sounding grunts and nonverbal communication that came up whenever she mentioned him.

As if her father was desperately trying to pretend that Mack didn't exist, which was just stupid. Her boyfriend was an upright, decent guy who didn't step on people's toes or do a lot of chest pounding. She certainly could've fared worse.

And as Mack uncurled himself from behind the seat of his truck and stepped toward her vehicle, Brooke eyed him up and down and considered she would've had to win the jackpot to have fared better.

Damn, the man was a looker. Dark hair, broad shoulders. A hint of five o'clock shadow dusted his chin and cheeks, and the sensual curve to his strong mouth promised mischief.

He pulled open her door. "Valet service."

"Yeah, right. You just want to drive my truck."

His gaze fell to her lips. He stepped in close enough to twist her toward him then slid her hips to the front of the seat. The move put her legs on either side of his body, and as their torsos touched, a soft moan escaped his lips. "There's a hell of a lot of things I want to drive, and your truck would only be one of them."

A shiver went up her spine. "No fair getting my motor

going. You've got volunteer firefighters on rotation at the hall tonight, don't you?"

Mack eased closer, sliding his cheek against hers and breathing deeply as if soaking in her scent. He pressed his lips to her neck, kissing up to the sweet spot behind her ear and making her shiver again. "We can find a place to be alone, but first we have an appointment with a very nice couple who are eager to say hello."

She cupped his face in her hands, twisting until she could kiss him properly. Mouth-to-mouth, torsos in contact.

Mack took control, still gentle but definitely in charge as he nibbled on her bottom lip. His hands gripped her tightly, thumbs rubbing back and forth along the waistline of her jeans, and Brooke once again considered the folly of being nearly thirty and living in far too close proximity to her father.

Not that it had stopped them completely. Mack was far too sexy to resist, and considering she was an adult, she had every right to bring home whomever she wanted.

Until this past year, she had rarely bothered.

God, his mouth was driving her wild. He stood there stoking her libido to high, as if they didn't have anywhere else to be, in spite of his earlier comment. It was as if he was trying to torment her and himself at the same time, because when they finally broke apart, foreheads resting together, his moan of frustration reverberated all the way to her toes.

"This is killing me," he muttered before stepping back. Holding out a hand to guide her down from the bench seat. "Okay. Operation Old-Fashioned begins in earnest. Let's get going before I do something that gets us arrested."

Brooke slipped her fingers into his. His hand curled around hers, big and protective. Cold wind moved against them from the north, but the sky was robin-egg blue, and the sun sparkled on the snow like a million fairies were dancing against the field of white. A magical path to walk en route to the double front doors of the seniors lodge.

"I haven't been here for a long time," she admitted guiltily.

"Your grandparents died a while ago, didn't they?"

"Two years ago for Grandpa. About four for my Gram." They were approaching the front stairs, the sidewalks completely clear of snow and ice. "We used to visit on a regular basis, but once they were gone, it was a lot harder to keep coming."

Even though there were people here who had been important in her grandparents' lives, the connections had grown fainter.

She and Mack went through the door and into the warmth. Before she could head to the check-in desk, he tugged her to the side of the hall. Strong fingers lifted her face to his, his gaze examining her.

He spoke softly, affection in his tone. "You don't need to feel as if you've done something wrong. You're a kind, loving individual, and while you might not have been *here* doing that caring, trust me; you have a lot of friends who would tell you thanks for all you've done in their lives."

He was right, but it still felt strange to be coming back into this familiar place after having been gone for so long.

"Thanks." She lifted up on her toes quickly and kissed him before guiding him to reception.

There was no one behind the desk, but as Brooke reached for the buzzer, someone stepped out of the resource room.

The woman moved forward briskly, patting her dark hair into place. Her eyes snapped with intelligence and a ready smile curled her lips. "Can I help you?"

"I'm Brooke Silver. My grandparents used to live here." Brooke glanced down the hallway as the sound of laughter rang in the distance. "I called earlier this week to see if there was anyone who knew them still in residence. I also have a recipe I hope someone can take a peek at and give me a translation."

The woman nodded. "I heard you would be stopping in. Come on, I'll take you to the common room. I think everybody you need to talk to is there right now anyway. It's tea and cookies time."

"I haven't seen you before. Are you new on staff?" Mack's fingers were still tangled with Brooke's as they headed down the pristine white linoleum.

The woman shook her head. "Volunteer. My grandparents live in the home. I've just moved into the community. Name's Yvette."

"Mack Klassen." He offered a hand. "Local firefighter."

Yvette shook his hand and then Brooke's as she offered her response. "Veterinarian."

"Oh, I've heard about you," Brooke said eagerly. "You're joining Josiah Ryder at his clinic."

"It's a great job, and he's a great boss. So far," she said jokingly. "What's your brand of mischief?"

"Mechanic."

Yvette nodded briskly. "Perfect. I need to get your number before you leave because my car got me here, but it's living on a prayer."

The main room of the lodge was full of small round tables with comfortable chairs around them. Half the tables had two or three people sitting at each of them, cups of hot liquid in front of the occupants and plates of icebox cookies and date squares set smack-dab in the middle for sharing.

Yvette crooked a finger and led them to one side. "There's someone here who wanted to speak with you."

Inside her heart, a pulse of happiness flared as Brooke glanced over to discover two familiar faces. Their hair was a little more silver, or maybe there was a little less of it, but the smiles were the same as all the times when she'd stopped in to visit with her grandparents. "Mr. and Mrs. Wright. How wonderful to see you both."

Geraldine Wright made a soft little noise that was probably as much of a squeal of delight as she would allow. "Sweet little Brooke. Come. Tell us everything you've been doing. And you know you're old enough to call us by our first names."

Her husband, Floyd, pushed back his wheelchair and held out a hand to Mack. "Who's this fine gentleman?"

"You know Mack," Geraldine said with a laugh. "It's okay if you don't remember, Floyd, but that's the nice fireman who comes in to do our fire drills."

Mack had taken Floyd by the hand and was shaking it briskly. "You're looking good today, sir. Have you had a chance to grab a cup of coffee and a cookie yet?"

Floyd looked confused for a moment but then smiled. "A cookie sounds like a great idea. Especially if they have chocolate in them."

There was a soft touch on her shoulder, and Brooke turned to discover Yvette watching her carefully. "It seems my grandparents know you."

"Geraldine and Floyd are your grandparents?" Brooke glanced back at the couple who were chatting with Mack as if the three of them were bosom buddies. She glanced at the other woman. "They were my grandparents' best friends. Since my grandpa died, I haven't been visiting the home as often."

The other woman tipped her chin slowly. "I've lived in Saskatchewan for most of my life, so I'm basically just getting to know them. Do you mind if I stick around while you talk?"

"Not at all." Brooke had to look away, a rush of emotions hitting her. "I came looking for some information to organize something special for Christmas. I didn't realize how many memories it was going to bring back."

"Memories are a good thing. I need to make more of them." Yvette lowered her voice. "My parents were estranged from

Mormor and Morfar. I'm choosing to remake the connection while there's still time."

It was kind of like hitting Brooke over the head with an oversized branch. "Yeah. I'm sort of in the same place." She smiled as best she could then gestured to the table. "Let's grab a couple more chairs. I'd love for you to join us, and I definitely need to get your number before I leave."

~

OVER THE YEARS, Mack had lived in many places and seen many things. As a military brat, he'd been hauled back and forth across the country. As a soldier, he'd travelled overseas for active duty. Through it all, he had learned a few hard truths, but the one hitting him square between the eyes today made him smile.

Men of a certain age had a universal ability to make him square his shoulders and mind his p's and q's.

Even as he was aware of Brooke and the conversation she was having with the veterinarian, Mack kept his gaze fixed on Floyd Wright. The old man offered a rambling story that stalled midsentence when he decided the cookie plate needed his attention.

Geraldine leaned forward on the other side, her nose wrinkling as she smiled at Mack. "It's good of you to stop in. You won't be setting off the fire alarms today, though, will you?"

Mack shook his head. "No, ma'am. Once-a-month drills only, and I was here last week."

"That's good," she said, pointing a finger out at the wintry day. "I know it's sunny, and I wouldn't want to give up my Alberta blue skies, but it's colder than a witch's tit right now."

He kept his expression as blank as possible, immensely amused at the same time.

Brooke slid another chair to the table, and she and Yvette joined them.

"You know the Wrights?" he asked Brooke.

She nodded then tilted her head toward Yvette. "It seems we've got that six-degrees-of-separation thing happening. Geraldine and Floyd were a couple of my grandparents' best friends, and Yvette is their granddaughter."

"Small towns. It's always exciting to discover what kind of tangled relations unfold." He spoke to Yvette. "I help run regular fire drills here at the lodge and chip in on other community events. Your grandparents are always the life of the party."

"I just don't dance as well as I used to," Floyd announced, leaning toward Brooke and patting his wheelchair. His eyes twinkled. "Not very light on my feet."

The next few minutes were filled with talk about everything from dances to the expected arrival of wild winter weather to a full-on conversation about what was going to be served for supper at the lodge.

Mack joined in on occasion, but mostly he watched as the two women bantered with the older couple, all of them working in unison when Floyd forgot what they were discussing. None of them made a fuss over it, just slid on to the next topic.

Then Brooke brought out the photo album.

Geraldine clasped her hands together and her eyes lit up with delight as they began flipping through pages. "I don't know all these people, but my goodness, Sharon was a looker."

Brooke caught Mack's eye and mouthed the words *my grandmother*.

Mack was in the middle of nodding in acknowledgement when a strange sensation washed over him, and he leaned back in his chair and tried to figure out what it was.

Couldn't be discomfort from visiting the lodge. Heck, he'd

talked to this very couple before, but there was something in this moment that seemed as if he'd opened up a window and was looking out for the first time.

Yvette was earnest and interested, leaning in to listen carefully when her grandparents spoke. Brooke laughed in response to something, her hand resting on his thigh as if them being there together was an ordinary, everyday thing.

It was.

And it wasn't.

An uneasy sensation tickled his gut, but he pushed it away and focused on what was going on now because *this* was important. "You have a chance to ask them anything about your holiday plans?" he encouraged Brooke.

She straightened, turning to a different section in the photo album and offering Geraldine a wink. "How's your Swedish?"

The old woman laughed louder than seemed appropriate considering the question. Then a stream of what obviously was not English poured from her lips, melodious and sharp.

Brooke smiled. "Well, that answers the question. Can you still read it?"

Geraldine sniffed. "My goodness. Of course I can still read it." She tapped her chest, then her lap and the top of her head before turning to Yvette sheepishly. "Perhaps I could read it better if I had my glasses. I think I left them in our room."

Yvette rose to her feet. "I'll grab them for you, Mormor."

She took off quickly down one of the long hallways.

Geraldine waited until Yvette was out of earshot, then twisted and caught Brooke's hand. "I like that girl, but I think she's lonely. She arrived in Heart Falls last week. I think she's spent more time with us old folks than she has with anyone else."

The old woman's gaze shifted to Mack, and she eyed him with a narrowed gaze. He didn't move, not sure what the old woman was up to.

She sniffed. "Since you're already spoken for, do you know any other nice men we could introduce her to?"

He stifled a laugh. Grandmother matchmaking services had kicked into high gear. "I make it my business to keep out of women's dating lives. The organizing of them, that is. I find it healthier."

Brooke was trying hard to not snicker and completely failing. "Mrs. Wright. I plan to introduce Yvette to my friends, but you should probably let her figure out the whole finding-a-guy part on her own. I mean, if that's what she's interested in."

"Oh, I know she likes boys," Geraldine offered eagerly. "I told her when she was talking about coming to visit us that it was okay if she brought her special someone, boyfriend or girlfriend. We're very progressive that way. Or at least I am, and Floyd is most of the time. When he remembers."

Yvette had reappeared in the hallway and was closing in on what was a very awkward conversation.

"Perhaps we can just let that idea go for now, and you can take a look at the recipe and see if you can translate it for us," Brooke suggested.

Notebook in hand, and prompting Geraldine firmly a few times to keep her on topic, they ended up with three different cookie recipes, a stew, and something that sounded like fruit porridge.

By this time, Floyd was nodding off.

Mack offered to take him back to his room. "If that's okay with you," he checked with Geraldine.

She hemmed hard a few times, obviously tempted by the opportunity to chat more. But she shook her head. "Not that I don't trust you, but I should go have a rest as well. And Floyd gets upset if I'm not with him when he wakes up." She glanced at Yvette. "If you could help us back to our room, I'd appreciate it."

"I'd love to help." Yvette gestured to Brooke's notebook. "Let me give you my number so you can text me the information for your shop."

It took a few minutes to leave the seniors lodge. Mack stopped to speak to the residents who recognized him. Brooke stayed at his side, fingers linked with his, and that strange sensation he'd felt earlier returned.

They were both quiet as they headed down the sidewalk toward their vehicles, caught up in their own heads. Still, he wasn't ready to let the day end. He tugged her hand to get her attention. "Supper?"

Another unreadable expression crossed her face, but she nodded slowly. "Want to come to my place?"

Which is how they ended up climbing the stairs to her apartment.

There was a note on the table from her father.

Gone to Rough Cut with the guys for a burger and a game of pool. Don't wait up.

Brooke hauled out the fixings for spaghetti. Mack dug in the fridge until he found what he needed to put together a salad.

They worked together, chatting about their most recent work activities. But when they settled at the table with full plates in front of them, he figured it was time to get the rest of the information he needed.

"Tell me again about your grandparents," Mack invited. She looked up, confusion in her eyes, and he pushed forward. "You've told me parts before, and you've been talking about your holiday memories, but it's been in bits and pieces. Put the whole story together so I have it all in my head as we do this thing."

She chuckled. "You're making me do a mission briefing, aren't you?" But she nodded slowly, eyes going dreamy as she began. "My birth mother wasn't thrilled at being a parent. She left when I was about two, and Dad ended up raising me by himself. Grandpa was a mechanic as well, and Gram was working in an accounting office. Dad moved home to reduce expenses and to get some extra help, but he didn't just drop me on them. He did the hard work, and they were there as backup. Except they loved having both of us around—I remember that pretty clearly. But they were *grandma* and *grandpa*. For the real decisions about what went on in my life, Dad called the shots."

"Makes sense that all three of them have big places in your memories."

Brooke nodded. "Gram and Grandpa spoiled me a little, and they had wild expectations of what they thought I should do with my life, but they never once told Dad that he needed to do anything different in the way he raised me."

"You never had any other women involved in your life? Like women that your dad dated?" Mack watched as she shook her head. "Or did you just not know about him dating?"

"He might have, but I doubt it. I know he hasn't in the last ten years when I would've been a lot more aware of that kind of thing. Seems as if we've always been enough. Me, Dad, Gram, and Grandpa. We didn't need anybody else."

Which wasn't exactly what Mack had hoped to hear.

Brooke's independence was something he found hugely attractive, but it made it tough to imagine she was waiting for him to come along and sweep her into a new, deeper relationship.

They cleaned up the table, and while Mack had the entire evening off, the *something strange on the air* sensation made it so he didn't simply crowd her toward her bedroom.

He wanted her—absolutely. Always, and fervently. But tonight it didn't seem right to focus on the physical pleasure between them. Or at least, not that type of physical pleasure.

"Come here," he ordered before hauling her toward the

couch and settling her between his knees so he could give her a back rub.

The groan that escaped as she leaned her neck to one side was dangerous on so many levels. "You have magic fingers."

"The magic is all yours, but only if you promise not to make that noise again," Mack warned. "No fair getting us riled up with nowhere to go."

She tilted her head a little more, mischief in her eyes. "I can orgasm right here, you know."

"Not from my hands on your neck. Not unless you've got some kink you've been holding back from me."

Brooke twisted on the floor, resting her hands on his thighs. "We could go to my room. Your hands are welcome to venture other places."

Temptation. Red-hot temptation.

Accompanied by a knock of reality. She'd said they were always in a hurry, and he knew why. They'd been stealing moments together for a long time, and it always felt as if they had to rush before they were interrupted.

That needed to change.

He leaned forward and kissed her nose, swaying away when she snickered. "You have a thing about my coworkers catching us fooling around. I have a thing about looking your dad in the eye after I've had my wicked way with you."

She nodded as she knelt higher, hands running over his shoulders and pulling him against her for a tight squeeze. "Damn those inexplicable dredges of teenage guilt that linger hard enough to mess with our fun."

Mack whirled through a series of ideas. He could plan a getaway. Book a fancy room at a big resort and, at some point, drop to one knee and pull out the ring.

Whether that should be before or after the first session of sex left them sated was still up for debate. He was leaning toward after—she'd be happy and relaxed after he'd worked her over from top to bottom and encouraged a lot more of those moans to escape her sexy lips.

A soft chuckle pulled him back to reality, and he stared into her bright eyes.

"You're thinking sex thoughts," she accused him. "Not fair to take action off the agenda then offer me sex eyes filled with sex thoughts."

"What exactly do my sex eyes do?" he teased.

Her voice dropped lower. "Make me hot. All over."

Mack shuddered, the ache inside him rock solid and pulsing with need. "I need to go shovel the walk. Or maybe the entire parking lot. Without a coat."

It was Brooke's turn to laugh, cupping his cheek gently then rising to her feet and hauling him after her. "No sex, no sex eyes. No more planning for holiday madness. Come and let me beat you at cards."

A couple hours later, they'd switched to watching a show together, curled up innocently on the couch. Brooke's head rested on his chest and she felt so damn perfect in his arms he was on the verge of blurting out a proposal before he reined it in.

How lame would that have been? Watching *Antiques Roadshow* then proposing?

Making memories was a hell of a lot of work.

Just before eleven, she finally kicked him out. "I have an appointment dropping off their vehicle before six-thirty."

After one final luscious kiss, Mack was making his way down the steps when the outside door opened and Gary stepped through. They stared at each other awkwardly for a moment, the stairs too narrow to pass each other safely.

Then Brooke's father sighed heavily and turned aside to let Mack pass.

Mack was so close to simply demanding to know what the hell was wrong, but he couldn't bring himself to be that rude.

Not now. Not after hearing over and over this evening how much this man had sacrificed and given for Brooke. How much he'd loved her.

Instead Mack forced a smile into his voice. "Good evening with the guys?"

"Won ten bucks."

"Better than the alternative." Mack adjusted his coat before nodding firmly. "I'll see you around."

He headed out the door and all the way into his truck without looking back once, but he could feel it; Gary's gaze was pinned between his shoulders.

Mack started his engine and backed away from the garage, glancing over to discover the blind on the window closing and the lights turning out as if Brooke's father had just stepped away.

Anticipation. Hesitation. Something unknown hovering on the wind. Whatever was waiting, Mack was getting antsy for it to hurry up and arrive.

4

The house at Lone Pine ranch was decorated from the front door to the tip of the roof with brightly coloured lights and swooping evergreen branches.

Inside, the scent of cinnamon and sugar was strong enough to send anyone into a Christmasy mood. Add in the delighted laughter of two little girls, and it was clear that holiday joy was alive and well in the warm family home her friend Hanna had created with Brad Ford.

Hanna's little girl, Crissy, darted underfoot, and Brooke pulled to a stop to keep from stepping on her or the other small participant joining in to help fulfill her first old-fashioned Christmas assignment. Talia Zhao was only slightly taller than Hanna, but just as eager to chatter, and the sound of little-girl voices filled the warm country kitchen.

"Okay, girls. Time to get baking if we want to be finished before Talia's daddy comes to pick her up." Hanna looped an apron over her head and pointed to the pile on the table. "Get yourself into one and I'll show you where to scoop up your ingredients."

It took a little longer to get started than just tying on aprons because Crissy and Talia had to decide what type of cookies they were going to make. Brooke already had her grandmother's recipe lined up and waiting, but first it was time for the excitement of choosing between gingersnaps and sugar cookies.

Eventually Hanna pulled Brooke aside, leaving the girls to deal with the ingredients alone, to Brooke's horror.

"They're going to have flour everywhere," Brooke warned.

Hanna's eyes shone as she nodded. "I imagine they will, but they'll have a wonderful time doing it."

Brooke shrugged. "Your home. Your disaster area."

"Trust me, I plan to stay close to the person who could cause the most damage." Hanna grinned, mischief in her eyes. "Neither of the girls have a reputation for burning things."

"I'm devastated." Brooke pressed a hand to her chest before offering her own smile in return. "Face it. I've been messing around in the kitchen for a lot longer than them. That's why my reputation is so impressive."

"It's a good thing you're dating a firefighter, that's all I'm saying."

An hour later there were cookies on every surface in the kitchen. The girls had flour on their faces and cookie crumbs at the corners of their mouths, but their eyes were wide with happiness as they rolled out the final batch.

Hanna and Brooke had finished assembling her Gram's cookies. It hadn't been as easy as Brooke remembered, but with Hanna's patient guidance, there was a cookie sheet in the oven that smelled heavenly.

Hanna paused to help Crissy pour glasses of milk for herself and Talia. When she returned, she leaned in and lowered her voice. "How are things between you and Mack?"

"Great," Brooke said eagerly. "He's helping me with some Christmas plans."

"Oh, really?" Hanna asked.

"Nothing nearly as shiny as what you've got set up," Brooke offered with a wink. "We've got these cookies to figure out, and some music and decorations, but otherwise it'll just be Christmas as usual with Dad. Mack will be there. Pretty quiet, really."

Hanna looked as if she was fighting to keep from saying something.

"What?"

There was a bit of headshaking that went on, and a quick moment of helping wipe up a spill from the girls before Hanna returned and looked Brooke squarely in the eye. "Do you like him?"

"Mack?"

Hanna nodded.

Here they went again. The impossible-to-answer questions all hinting at the same thing. What tack should she take this time?

"Yes," Brooke drawled. "Is there a reason why I shouldn't?"

Hanna looked horrified. "No, of course not. He's wonderful. I mean he *seems* wonderful, and it seems as if he's wonderful to you. And Brad thinks the world of him."

Rambling. Definitely rambling. Brooke lifted a brow and stared at her friend.

Hanna rolled her eyes in great imitation of her daughter. "I can't believe you're not picking up on all my subtle hints," she complained.

"I can't believe you're trying for subtle when I just ate my weight in sugar."

Her friend laughed. "Okay, pretend I never asked because it's clear you want me to mind my own business."

"Maybe. Or maybe I really don't know what you're talking about. I have no intention of breaking up with him. He's a good guy, Hanna. He makes me happy. Helping me plan some fun stuff so that this Christmas rocks for my dad is pretty sweet."

"That's great, and I'm glad about all of that, but don't you want..."

That's when Hanna had to go to rescue the girls before the spritz cookies ended up squirted over the counter instead of onto the cookie sheet.

Brooke hurried over to help as well, and for a moment, wrangling sweet buttery goodness into the oven was a big enough distraction she didn't have to say anything else to her friend.

Because she did want more. Mack had stepped into her life and become such a solid part of it on a *when we can get together* kind of basis that the thought of not having him around seemed wrong.

When they'd first started seeing each other, she'd wondered if he was only going to be in town temporarily, but there'd been no talk of him leaving recently. In fact, she couldn't remember the last time he said anything about possibly having to move.

He was just...hers.

"Hello, the house."

A racket sounded from the front door. Masculine voices followed by Talia's and Crissy's cheers as they raced to greet their fathers.

"Look at the pretty cooks we found," Brad announced, tangling a hand around Crissy and marching forward until he could include Hanna in his hug. "The place smells wonderful."

"We made lots of cookies, Daddy," Talia informed her father as Ryan stepped into the room, Mack right behind him.

"It looks as if we're going to need lots of cookies," Brooke teased. "Good to see you again, Ryan. How are things down at the pub?"

"Not bad. I'm selling warm winter drinks faster than the beer these days." He picked up Talia and held her close, rubbing their noses together. "Have you been a good little chef for Hanna?"

She insisted she had then gestured toward the oven. "They're nearly done. We can have warm cookies soon."

Mack crossed the floor and stood beside Brooke. "Do you have warm cookies for me as well?" He waggled his brows and turned the question into something completely different.

Brooke wasn't the only one who offered a snort of amusement.

"Keep it PG," Brad warned softly.

"Just looking forward to nibbling on Brooke's sweet things in a bit," Mack said innocently, his hand sliding over her hip and pulling her against his body. "Hey, babe. How's Operation Old-Fashioned coming?"

"First attempt is in the oven, Captain," she told him, tugging his hand from where it had snuck under her shirt because his fingers against her bare belly were doing dangerous things to her insides. If they had any hopes of keeping things child-friendly, she couldn't have Mack teasing her to combustion.

He rumbled a complaint but eased away, and her heart rate slowed to nearly normal. They all moved around the kitchen, getting oven mitts ready. Ryan helped Brad gather more glasses of milk for the upcoming taste test.

Mentally, Brooke added a new item on her think-about list. She was working to make this a special Christmas for her father, but it felt very important to include Mack in that as well, beyond the part where she got his help and him being present for the actual day of celebration.

What would *he* truly want? Dare she try to set up something like a getaway without checking with him first?

They didn't get to spend nearly enough time together, especially not private time. And while getting naked with the man was high on her priority list, she also wanted to sit and talk without one or the other of them being pulled away. Without interruptions.

Only, the holidays were so full as it was, secretly planning to steal him away seemed impossible. The best she could hope for was to get Brad to pack a bag for his friend on the sly so she could tuck it away in case the opportunity arose.

Other than that, she'd have to wait until the new year like she'd thought before.

Sometimes the slow way was the only way.

The buzzer on the oven went off, pulling her thoughts back to the here and now. To the man watching her with a smile on his lips as addictive as the baked goods on the table.

THE PAST MINUTES had been a fantastic reminder for Mack of how lucky his best friend was. No sour taste of jealousy marred Mack's observations, but there was definitely a deep, strong pull of wanting to enjoy the same kind of goodness for himself.

Brad had found himself a beautiful woman who was kind and caring and visibly loved him. He had a daughter who had come ready-made into his world and a new life on the way. He had his father, a brother, and a whole pile of friends Mack knew well from constantly being dragged into the middle of activities.

It was a slice of paradise on earth. A picture that Mack wanted—only with him and Brooke in the starring roles. Not just the two of them together, but the family bit as well, and that realization was enough to leave him breathless.

"You guys are a little earlier than we expected." Hanna laid a cookie sheet on the cooling rack then offered the oven mitts to Brooke. "We thought you'd show up just in time for supper."

"The smell of cookies magically traveled all the way to us and made us hurry our meeting," Ryan teased. "Actually, Talia and I need to go see her grandparents tonight, and with the snow coming, I thought we'd leave a little early."

Two little girls heaved heavy sighs of disappointment, but he pointed to the plate of cookies and raised a brow. "Seems as if you made a good start on the holidays already."

Talia nodded slowly, her gaze darting between Crissy and Hanna over and over.

"I'm glad you've had a good time with your friend." Ryan tucked his fingers under his daughter's chin and spoke softly. "Nainai and Yeye are looking forward to seeing you, as well. But we don't need to leave for half an hour. And you and Crissy can play another day."

While Ryan dealt with his daughter, Hanna stepped beside Mack, leaning closer to speak quietly enough that Talia wouldn't overhear. "Will you stay for supper?" she asked. "There's plenty. Patrick's out in the barn, but he'll be back soon. We'd love to have you and Brooke join us."

He glanced at Brooke who nodded her agreement, and with that arranged, everyone settled around the big kitchen table for the taste test the girls insisted on.

"Do you really think we should do this?" Brad asked with mock seriousness. "Eat cookies just before dinner?"

At Mack's side, Brooke let out a choked noise that sounded like an attempt at holding back laughter. "You shouldn't think of it as eating cookies before dinner, but having leftover *dessert* cookies from lunch, since we've been at this off and on for the past two hours."

Brad laughed. "Well, I guess that makes it better."

Crissy and Talia demanded the sugar cookies get first taste. While they were a little misshapen, when the sugary goodness melted on his tongue, Mack couldn't resist making an appreciative noise.

The girls' faces lit up with joy.

"Santa is going to love those," he told them seriously.

Crissy dipped her chin knowingly. "He does. All his helpers love them too, especially…"

She glanced at Hanna then pressed her lips together. Hushing herself although she wiggled at the difficulty of staying mum on whatever wanted to spill free.

Beside him, Brooke laughed softly, obviously in on the secret. Her thigh rubbed his and something sweeter than the sugar he'd just consumed rushed him, and he was a second away from grabbing her and kissing her senseless.

Instead, he reached for the other plate on the table. A spicy scent rose from the square shapes decorated with beautiful pictures on the surface, and his mouth watered. "Are these your Gram's recipe?"

Brooke nodded. "Thanks to Hanna and the girls, I did not burn them."

Everyone at the table took one, ceremoniously lifting it to their mouths at the same time for the first bite.

First *difficult* bite. The square was more rock than cookie. And the taste—

Mack managed to keep from gagging or spitting it out.

Crissy and Talia were not quite as polite, reaching for their glasses of milk and downing them completely before looking with wide-eyed worry at Hanna.

Hanna placed her barely nibbled cookie back on her plate and faced Brooke with concern. "Not that I want to cast further doubt on your cooking abilities, but did you copy down the recipe correctly?"

Brooke made a rude noise. "Figures. I don't burn it, but it still tastes terrible."

"So, that's *not* what it's supposed to taste like? Good to know," Brad said.

Brooke stuck out her tongue at him, and Talia and Crissy both laughed, tension easing from the room.

"I suggest we all eat a gingersnap to recover from that…

whatever it was," Brooke said smoothly. "After all of you promise not to sue me for trying to poison you."

"And then it's time to clean up." Hanna passed around another plate before heading to the counter to finish tipping cookies into a bag. "These are for you and your grandparents, Talia."

Cookie munching and crumb swiping commenced, and in the confusion, Mack caught hold of Brooke's hand and tugged her with him toward the side of the house.

The air grew cooler the farther they moved away from the kitchen and wood-burning stove in the living room, but he had plans that would heat them both up plenty.

"I don't know what happened," Brooke complained. "I swear I had the recipe right—*oh!*"

He twirled her toward him and stepped closer. An instant later, her back sank into the thick coats hanging on the mudroom wall as he pinned her in place with his body.

Breasts soft against his torso, curvy hips tight to his. Mack caught her chin in his fingers and stared at her mouth hungrily for a long, intense moment before closing the distance between them.

He wanted to show her he could do slow—that she deserved to be worshiped—but aching desire made her impossible to resist.

The sweetness of her kiss had nothing to do with the cookies they'd eaten and everything to do with his addiction. He craved this. Needed her taste in his mouth, her scent in his system, her nails digging into his shoulders. Their tongues teased then retreated as he slowly rocked their hips together.

He was harder than those damn cookies had been, and that was saying something.

Mack adjusted position slightly, pulling her more firmly onto his thigh, and she gasped. He captured the sound with his mouth, lifting his leg and rubbing harder against her core.

A low rumble escaped him as she dragged her nails down his back. Lines of heat branding him and making him curse the layers of fabric between them. He wanted skin. Naked and wild under him. Open to his touch and his mouth and his teeth.

But since he couldn't have that at the moment, he'd take getting to see passion flare in her eyes and watching her come unglued. Undone by his touch and his presence.

He leaned in harder, captured her hips, and dragged her upward enough to get her on her tiptoes. No control on her part, all of it his. He stared intently as desire flushed her skin.

Voices carried from deeper in the house, but here in the small room there was just his heavy breathing and her low gasps. The sounds turned to trembling rasps before she bit her bottom lip and tried to silence her pleasure.

"You get off on it, don't you? Don't want to be overheard fooling around at the fire hall, but the chance we might accidentally be caught in some public place presses all your hot buttons, doesn't it?"

"Yours too," she pointed out with a low moan. "Thank you, Christmas spirits, and hallelujah."

He laughed softly because she was right. "I promise not to let anyone underage be traumatized by our wicked, wicked ways."

But he was definitely on board for finishing this round before he was forced to stop. Didn't mean he couldn't make a point, though. Mack slowed the upward motion of dragging her up his thigh.

She pounded a fist against his back in protest.

"*Noooo.* Don't stop," she whispered, desperation in her tone.

"You need more? You want more?" He pressed his lips next to her ear and let the words rumble against her skin. "You want *me*?"

"*Yes.*"

Mack dropped her back in position and set his leg in

motion, rubbing his thigh muscle against her sex like he was a Boy Scout working two pieces of dry kindling on a windy day.

Brooke twisted her face to the side, lips desperate to meet his as she quivered, then shuddered, then gasped. Her heart pounded hard enough that the echo of the pulse reverberated against his lips as he skimmed down the side of her throat, holding her up as she fought to catch her breath.

He was still hard, still aching and needy, but damn happy.

The door to outside swung open with a low creak.

Mack twisted instantly, Brooke slid a step away.

As Brad's father came through the door, she hurriedly hung the coats they'd been compressing a little more firmly on the hooks, as if that's all she and Mack had been up to. A little cleanup in the mudroom.

The fact she kept her back toward the other man to hide her flushed face and the wildly satisfied grin she wore amused Mack and proved how smart she was.

Distraction, now.

"Patrick. Good to see you again. Can I help with your coat?" Mack offered.

Patrick Ford leaned on his double canes for a moment, eyeing Brooke's industrious tidying before he nodded and let Mack take it from him. "Feel a little warm in here to you?"

Brooke coughed, then bent to straighten a pair of boots.

Mack dragged his gaze off her perfect ass and smiled at Mr. Ford. "Just the contrast from being outside, I imagine. It's a cold one out there."

"Cold, and there's snow on the way. The storms around here have a way of sneaking up on us, but if the predictions are right, this could end up the snowiest Christmas in ten years," Patrick told him. "Going to have to work hard to stay warm."

Staying warm wasn't their issue, Mack figured. Spontaneous combustion was more along the lines of what he and Brooke had to worry about.

She met his gaze as Patrick walked away, her cheeks rosy and her eyes bright.

Heat? They had it in spades. He needed to get moving on the part where he was granted the privilege to stoke her fires anytime he wanted.

It really was all he wanted for Christmas.

5

"Again."

A chorus of groans greeted his announcement, but Mack had already hit the timer before sending his skipping rope twirling into action.

In front of him, a half dozen volunteer firefighters were moving through the workout with as much enthusiasm as they could muster. The air carried the scent of sweat and ever-present lingering smoke, plus the rich aroma of tomato sauce as the second team, which was taking part in a first-aid refresher upstairs, worked on the communal meal they'd all share later.

Here by the fire equipment, music pounded around them, the heavy beat syncopated with the sound of feet against the concrete floor.

"Keep up," Mack encouraged. "Just a little more."

"You. Said. That. Before." A smart-ass quip was delivered in gasping breaths from one of the group as everyone pushed through until the timer went off.

Instantly the crew drooped, hands resting on knees as they breathed hard, but waited and watched, refraining from dropping to the floor in exhaustion. Mack clapped his hands in approval and offered them the words they'd been waiting for.

"That's it. Cool down and stretch before you hit the showers."

A collective sigh of relief rang out.

Mack wasn't the only one to chuckle. At his side, Alex gave his own announcement. "Dinner's on the table in forty-five. You've got time before hitting the grub line."

Mack gave final instructions. "Around the station five times, whatever speed you want, but the last two should be walking. And don't forget to stretch your deltoids as well as your hamstrings—those arms we did earlier in the day are going to kill if you don't."

The fatigued crew hauled themselves off the floor where they'd collapsed, shuffling good-naturedly into a pack to amble around the perimeter of the hall.

Alex tipped his head after them. "Set a good example and cool down yourself."

Mack nodded, jogging slowly as Alex joined him. "How did your session go?"

Alex shared what they'd managed to cover in terms of emergency response on the medical side. Mack nodded, pleased with how the evening had gone overall.

They'd been mixing up the training over the past while— a great idea brought in by one of their temporary EMTs. Having a strong volunteer force was about the camaraderie as much as the skills, but having them divide up physical training with technical refreshers meant if there were an emergency that evening, then the entire team wasn't going to be exhausted.

They'd completed enough laps, so Mack slowed to a march, nodding in approval as some of the volunteers from upstairs came to join in a huge, impromptu stretch session. "I'm impressed with how well the teams are getting along."

"It's great," Alex agreed. "I wonder if we need another lead coordinator, though."

Mack glanced at the other man. "You don't think the four of us are enough?"

"I think having backup who is trained and knowledgeable about the system is even better. Plus, I was thinking Brad shouldn't be considered one of our leads full-time anymore. Not with his responsibilities outside the area, and the new ones that will be coming on board this year."

Impressive. Mack nodded as he eyed Alex thoughtfully. "You're right. I hadn't considered the baby part of it. You have any ideas? Anyone you think of on the teams who is ready for more responsibility?"

"I've got a few ideas, but I thought I should put the bug in your ear. You should probably be the one to tell Brad he's being moved to a more supervisory role." Alex grinned widely. "Have fun with that."

Mack let his amusement show. "Trust me. Brad's not one to hold on to a job just for shits and giggles. He knows how much time it takes to be here and alert. Having a newborn in the house isn't very conducive to our chief being at his finest."

They slid into the group gathered in the open space beside the gleaming fire truck, joining in conversations and stretching, slipping out to the community shower room in small groups to wash away the sweat.

Mack had just finished dragging a comb through his hair when the sound of the dinner bell rang through the building.

The scent of chocolate hovered on the air, although the dessert table was still bare. The meal was all in place, though, and he joined the lineup to heap his plate with spaghetti and a rich meat sauce that had him drooling.

Then he stole the salad tongs from the volunteer in front of him who was distractedly checking her cell phone.

"Hey," Charity complained. "I wasn't done with those."

He dropped a serving on her plate before serving himself up twice as much. "You snooze you lose," he reminded her. "Just because phones aren't outlawed when training is done doesn't mean this is the time to be using one. You might get distracted and miss out on something good."

One of their younger recruits, Charity only rolled her eyes a little as she tucked the phone into her back pocket. "Yes, sir."

Fighting to keep the grin off his face was damn hard at times. Mack joined a different table of volunteers he hadn't spoken with in a while, listening to their stories and answering questions.

His plate was empty, and he was ready to go attack the trays of brownies now waiting on the dessert table when, in his back pocket, his phone vibrated.

Only a limited number of people in his contacts had alerts attached to their messages, Brooke being one of them.

Mack snuck the phone out and held it under the edge of the table to discreetly check his messages.

Brooke: *I found some boxes!*

Ten out of ten for sheer enthusiasm. Now all he had to do was figure out what the hell she was talking about.

Mack: *are these good boxes?*

Brooke: *very good boxes. Ones filled with Christmas decorations.*

Mack: *that's great. Anything useful?*

Brooke: *I'm not sure. Just because I found them doesn't mean I've been able to open them. Long story, but do you have time to come over later?*

Mack: *I'm done in a bit, and I'm not on call until tomorrow. I'd love to come check out your decorations.*

Brooke: *I don't know which emoji I should send you for that comment*

Mack: *let's avoid the whole vegetable/fruit debacle. I still haven't recovered from the time you sent me the eggplant emoji next to a bonfire. I swear I needed therapy.*

Brooke: *LOL. Get your eggplant and the rest of you over here whenever you can.*

The realization that the room had gone utterly quiet while he'd been distracted clicked in a split second before he shoved his phone in his pocket and looked up.

His plate was gone. His glass was gone. Every face at the table was turned toward him with an amused expression and raised brows.

Across the table from him, Charity dug her fork into a final bite of brownie, raising it toward her mouth and humming happily. "You know there's a time and a place for cell phones. You get distracted and you might miss out on something good."

Alex tipped the empty brownie pan toward him. "Sorry, bro."

"You snooze, you lose," Charity offered sweetly as laughter welled around the room.

Mack shook his finger at her but nodded good-naturedly. He'd set himself up for that one.

He was still smiling when he made it over to Brooke's. The bitter cold whirled around him as he made the short dash between his truck and the garage. He slid into the warmth, patting his arms firmly to knock the chill off his coat before reaching for her.

"I'll have you know I got in trouble because of you," he complained.

"Really?"

"Okay, it wasn't your fault, but I still think you should make it up to me. I missed out on brownies." He offered a mock pout.

"Then you shouldn't have been texting at the table," Brooke teased, stepping back as he jerked upright in shock. "Oh, I have my sources down at the fire hall. I know *everything*..."

Ignoring the fact that his coat was still icy cold, Mack chased after her, catching her in his arms and kissing her laughing lips firmly. Brooke banged on his shoulders in mock anger for a moment before thrusting her fingers into his hair and deepening the kiss.

By the time they stopped there was no more chill in the air.

She cupped his cheek with her hand. "All teasing aside, thanks for coming over. I found the jackpot of Christmas decorations. I think."

"That's very decisive. Not."

Brooke led him across the floor of the shop, weaving between parked trucks and lift equipment. She tugged him close as they passed tires and pressure valves, stopping in the far corner where an ancient ladder leaned against the wall, just barely reaching a platform a good sixteen to twenty feet over their heads.

Mack looked up, equal parts of horror and admiration rushing him. "Are you telling me you climbed this already?"

The ladder was sturdy enough—he supposed—but it wasn't something he'd have gone up without backup and maybe a safety line.

"I'm not stupid," Brooke said dryly. She wrinkled her nose adoringly. "Okay, I was borderline stupid until I realized you'd probably kill me if I didn't kill myself first. I have *not* gone up the ladder more than the first few rungs. Just far enough so I could lift my phone and take a close-up picture of the storage space. I don't think I've ever been up there."

"Because there's no access that doesn't require having wings or spider capabilities?"

"Because I wasn't interested enough to wonder," she admitted. "I'm enough of a neat freak that if I found a new area to organize, I'd have to deal with it. If I don't know it's there, it's less work."

Mack walked away from her, headed back to his truck. "You're the weirdest neat freak I know, but in this case, I'm thankful. Stay here. Both feet on the ground."

"Yes, cap."

By the time he was back with a rope from his truck, Brooke had cleared away the shop equipment in the area, giving him a clear path to set up safe passage.

He tossed one end of his backup rope over a metal girder, looping a figure eight into his climbing harness and tying off the far end around Brooke. "You remember how to do this?"

She nodded, adjusting her stance and holding the rope tucked around her back and under her arm so if he fell or the ladder failed, all she had to do was use her body weight to counterbalance him.

"Although I also remember the last time we did this, I wasn't heavy enough to keep you in the air."

"All you have to do is keep me from hitting the ground," he reminded her. He dropped a quick kiss on her lips. "Thanks for taking care of me."

"Thanks for going on a decoration treasure hunt," she returned as he made his way up the ladder.

The journey up was thankfully uneventful. The space at the top of the landing was wide enough for him to rest his hips, the metal platform secure and safe.

"I see your boxes," he announced. "Also what looks like

archery equipment, and enough spiderwebs to make Shelob proud."

"Ugh."

~

Brooke held firmly onto his lifeline, staring into the rafters. And while she wasn't terribly afraid of spiders, she was doubly thankful that she'd waited for Mack's help.

"No idea on the archery equipment," she told him. "You want to rig up a system to drop the boxes down?"

"Got it under control." He pulled a second rope from under his jacket and held it for her to see. "Give me a minute to retie my safety, then we'll set up a production line."

It took a good twenty minutes for them to get everything in place, but eventually an entire collection of boxes and wooden cutouts were leaning against the shop wall. The memories were flooding back far clearer.

"The candy canes had twinkling white and red lights—I remember those—and the deer looked as if they were leaping. One set of lights after the other would go on and off. This is *fantastic*." She peered up at where he was coiling the rope he'd used to lower everything to the ground. "I can't wait to go through it all."

"Let's get me down first, then we can tuck stuff away before your dad gets back."

She glanced at her watch. "He shouldn't be home for hours. The hockey game is on, and we don't have a channel."

Mack talked her through the safety rope again, making sure she was set up properly before he twisted off the platform and put his feet back on the admittedly delicate ladder.

Of course, he'd only taken a couple of steps downward when the man door opened, blistering winter weather whirling in along with her father.

Brooke only spared him a momentary glance before turning her full attention back on Mack. She was going to have to bluster through and pretend they weren't up to anything, although the decorations were all in plain sight. "Hey, Dad. Be with you in a minute."

Soft cursing rang out, followed by the sound of her father's feet slapping across the concrete floor. His breathing was ragged, but he didn't say anything. Just stood beside her silently while Mack made his way down the ladder.

But the instant her boyfriend's feet hit the ground, her dad exploded. "Are you out of your goddamn mind? What the hell do you think you're doing?"

Mack frowned at her father's outburst, sliding closer as if to protect her.

Brooke figured she had to be blinking like a deer frozen in headlights. "We were looking for decorations. What's wrong?"

Gary swung his hands in the air, his mouth open, an unreadable expression in his eyes. "You just— I can't—"

He finished with an incomprehensible roar, as if he were frustrated and furious at the same time.

"It's okay," Mack said easily, his tone moderated and reassuring. "I was roped in, and we'll get this mess out of your way—"

"You'll get it the hell out of here. I don't want to see it. *None of it.*" Gary's hands shot out as if he were pushing the entire lot over the edge of a cliff. "I can't believe you'd be so *stupid*. Just... get it out of here."

He spun and stomped away, steam nearly visibly rising from him.

Brooke watched in utter confusion. Okay. That was completely unexpected.

She twisted back to discover Mack wore an expression that matched the sensation in her gut.

He met her gaze. "So. That went well."

"I have no idea what just happened," she admitted. "I guess the decorations were not a good idea? Is it possible I was wrong about this whole thing?"

Mack stared at the door her father had disappeared behind. He shook his head thoughtfully. "The only thing that's clear is we're missing some information. Let's not jump to any conclusions. See if he says something more to you in the next while."

"Yeah. Let's hope he opens with 'hey, let me explain why I just lost my shit.'"

He laughed softly, sliding in next to her to help undo the ropes that still anchored them together. "You never know. In the meantime, if we're going to be able to use them, I need to adjust the lighting strands on the bigger decorations to cheaper LEDs the way Rose suggested. Let's put everything in my truck for now and I'll take a look. If there's anything I'm not sure about, I'll take a picture and send it to you."

She nodded slowly, but as they worked together to clear the dozen or so boxes and other items from the shop, it wasn't with the sense of satisfaction she'd hoped to have at this point.

Her great plans for this old-fashioned Christmas were off to a terrible beginning, and she hadn't a clue why.

6

Music played softly in the background, but more important was the scent of buttered popcorn and something savory that hit Brooke's nose the instant she walked into Tansy and Rose's apartment for their monthly girls' night out.

"Oh my God, what do I smell?" Brooke shrugged out of her coat and hung it on the wall with the others already there before hurrying across to join the party.

Smiling faces greeted her from the kitchen area.

"Oh, this? Just a cheese fondue with aged cheddar and extra wine," Rose offered.

"And fresh baked French bread. Get over here before we start without you," Tansy demanded.

There were two others at the table as well. Hanna pulled back the chair beside her, patting the seat. "Saved you a spot."

"Stop being a suck-up," Tansy teased. "We're missing a whole bunch of the girls, so there's plenty of room."

"But we have a special new person to replace them. Hi, Yvette. Good to see you." Brooke dropped into the chair beside Hanna. "Are these guys treating you right?"

Yvette's shy smile took in the other three women. "They let me have first pick of the cookies. Almond-filled shortbread. I feel very warm and welcome."

A full wine glass was pressed into Brooke's hand. Rose offered her a wink along with an empty plate. "She doesn't know we're softening her up for the interrogation later."

Yvette straightened slightly, a touch of worry in her expression as she glanced at Brooke. "I suppose a little bit of friendly interrogation is okay. It *was* a good cookie."

Tansy placed the cheese pot on top of the flame then handed around the basket of bread chunks. "To holiday eating, which totally doesn't count and has no calories because it's holiday-based. Or something like that."

"Hear, hear." Hanna raised her glass of water in the air. "I like having a reason to excuse the extra calories."

Brooke tore off a piece of bread from the still warm loaf, humming happily as she lifted it to her nose and took a deep breath. "Damn, that's amazing. Tansy, will you marry me?"

"Don't ask questions you don't want an answer to," Rose warned. "With how bad her luck is with vehicles, being married to a mechanic would be right up her alley."

Tansy waved a hand in the air. "Yes, true. But I don't poach, and the delectable Ms. Silver seems thoroughly taken by a certain hunky hottie." She leaned forward, her eyes bright as she examined Brooke intently. "Speaking of hunky hotness, Yvette was telling us the two of you have been seen everywhere around town."

"Not everywhere," Yvette protested. She frowned. "I mean, I mentioned I saw you together at the lodge, and the shop when I dropped off my car for the tune-up. And at the fire hall when I stopped in to grab the info the vet office needed."

"Plus Buns and Roses, and the bar, and the sporting goods shop," Rose added.

"When did you see us at the sporting goods shop?" Brooke

asked in confusion. "We haven't been in there since the summer."

The other women all laughed. Brooke smiled sheepishly.

"Skipping to a different topic than speculating endlessly about Brooke and her hottie. *Yvette...*" Tansy turned her gaze on the newcomer who was dipping a piece of bread into the cheese to scoop up a hearty serving. "New in town. New job, new outlook on life."

Yvette waited until she'd finished chewing her mouthful then raised a brow. "Was there a question in there, somewhere?"

Brooke snorted. "Excuse me. That was the perfect response, though. Welcome to dealing with Tansy."

Across the table, her friend slowly lifted her right hand before unfurling her middle finger. Laughter swelled.

Tansy shook her head. "I'm so misunderstood. No, Yvette, here's the question. What do *you* think about Brooke and her hottie?"

More snickers from Hanna and Rose. Yvette grinned in amusement as Brooke debated whether she wanted to waste a piece of her bread and throw it at Tansy's head.

"Don't answer that, Yvette. Tell us how things are going with your grandparents. And how are you liking the job at the veterinary clinic?"

"The clinic is great. Josiah's great to work for, and he's giving me lots of freedom. I'm going out to the local ranches with him to get to know everybody, which has been kind of fun."

Chatter continued, just general discussion, until Yvette brought the topic back to sharing her thoughts regarding Heart Falls.

"It's smaller than I expected," Yvette admitted. "I'm not sure if this is somewhere I want to stay long term, but then that's kind of silly considering I always figured I'd end up working independently on a ranch, which is kind of like the ultimate small town. Everybody knows *everything* about everyone else."

"Heart Falls people can be a lot more in your face than is pleasant at times," Hanna said softly, "but then again, that closeness also means there are always people around willing to help when you need it. That's pretty special."

Brooke nodded. "I've lived in Heart Falls all my life. I've visited other places, and I lived in Calgary when I went to get my training, but this is where I want to be long term."

"You're going to grow old here?" Tansy asked.

"Probably." Brooke left the other things unsaid for now. The parts that would hopefully come *before* the getting old happened. The bits about home and hearth and family.

Or she intended to ignore that part of the conversation, but her friends were like bloodhounds on a mission. The attack came from the least expected quarter.

"Sounds as if you're ready to settle down," Yvette offered innocently. "Maybe you and that hottie of yours should do something about that."

A chorus of snickers rose from Hanna, Tansy, and Rose.

"I told you she'd fit right in," Brooke said dryly before turning her attention to Yvette. "Right now, the biggest thing I'm worried about is trying to figure out how to get this Christmas to turn out the way it's supposed to. So far, everything's still falling apart instead of falling into place."

"Did you get that recipe checked?" Hanna asked. "To see if it was copied down wrong?"

Brooke pulled the recipe card out of her pocket where she'd taken to worrying at it in her spare time. "The details were right, but it doesn't work. Obviously—you were inflicted by the results. I even tried once more at home, and they tasted just as bad."

She shook her head. The cookies were one thing, but

adding on her dad's strange over-the-top reaction to the decorations the other night?

The only good part was Mack hadn't seemed upset. He'd carried on, solid and understanding. He kept moving forward, kept trying, in spite of the stupid mix-up or whatever had triggered her father.

So...*Mack.*

She hadn't figured out what she was going to give him for Christmas, and after her talk about keeping it homemade, she needed to get her act together, and soon.

A tug on her sleeve dragged her attention from her meandering thoughts. Rose and Tansy were chattering near the sink about something as they refilled drinks, but Yvette and Hanna were both watching her closely.

"I meant it as a tease, but I'm sorry if my comment was out of line," Yvette said softly.

Brooke waved her apology away. "You were fine. I'm the one who's out of sorts, which is not your fault."

"I'll apologize as well," Hanna slipped in. "You know I want the best for you, but there's absolutely no rush. If there's anything we can do to help you find your happiness, we will, but the timing is up to you."

And yet that was part of the problem. If Brooke had her way, she and Mack would already be a full-time couple. But they couldn't before—the timing had been wrong. And now, with just two weeks to go until Christmas, it seemed silly that she suddenly wanted to push the agenda.

"I still remember how thrilled my Grandpa was when Gram surprised him with just the right present. Nothing big and ostentatious, but perfect for him. It was proof of the special bond between them, how she knew exactly what would make him the happiest." Brooke wasn't sure why she was sharing this, but the earnest expression on both their faces pulled the softly spoken confession free. "I want to see that look on Mack's face.

I want to prove what we've got between us is *more* than just comfortable."

Happiness pooled in Hanna's eyes. "Then don't rush. You've got this one, Brooke. I know you do. And when it's right, he's going to grab on tight and never let you go."

Yvette's expression was serious but happy. "You guys are good together. That part is clear to see. Even from a newcomer's point of view."

Yet Brooke wanted more than just "good together." She wanted the kind of connection shown to her over a lifetime by her grandparents.

Tansy and Rose returned to the table and the conversation faded away, a quiet secret between the three of them. A quiet promise that if Brooke needed help, she would have it, like the best possible small-town gift.

~

ANNOYANCE BUZZED LIKE OUT-OF-CONTROL FIRECRACKERS. Mack dragged a hand through his hair and stomped the distance between his bunk and the kitchen at the fire hall.

Two remaining volunteers sat at the dining table, working on something. Ryan was a few chairs down from them, flipping through a uniform catalogue as the kettle slowly worked up to a full whistle on the counter. Mack unplugged it, grabbing a cup then placing it on the counter a little harder than was good for the porcelain. It cracked in multiple pieces, shards flying.

Mack swore.

"Don't move," Ryan ordered. He had the broom out a minute later, the debris from the accident cleared out of sight before Mack was finished growling in frustration.

A second cup appeared beside him, the kettle as well, then Ryan twisted to lean against the counter, arms folded over his chest.

"You want to try that again with a little less enthusiasm?" Ryan deadpanned.

"Thanks." Mack stirred himself a cup of hot cocoa, offering his friend a tired smile along with one of the monster-sized chocolate chip cookies that had shown up at the fire hall. A gift from some member of the community. "I'm a bit of a grump tonight."

Ryan twisted away and made himself a cup of tea. "Since you're off work yet still hanging around here, Brooke must be otherwise occupied for the evening."

"Girls' night out."

"I bet your ears are burning." Ryan grinned. "I assume that's what they do at these nights. Talk about their guys."

Mack wasn't going to assume. "Chances are high they're dirt-talking everyone in town, including you."

"Me? What did I do?" Ryan pressed a hand to his chest as if he were utterly innocent.

"You're male. You're single. There's got to be something you've done wrong recently." Mack winked. "Nah, I figure we're low on their priority list for talking about at this time of year. Probably more tied up in holiday plans. Speaking of which, what's the best homemade gift you've ever gotten?"

Ryan blinked at the change of topic. "Talia."

"Seriously? Her birthday is on Christmas day?"

His friend nodded. "Other than that, there was a picture that Justina gave me the first year we were married. I like it better than our wedding pictures. Just an ordinary moment, but we looked so damn happy together..."

His voice faded, and Mack didn't push. He knew Ryan's wife had passed away a number of years ago, but it had to still hurt.

"Are you trying to come up with something good for Brooke?" Ryan asked.

"Something homemade," he acknowledged. "A picture could work."

His friend sat beside him at the long table, far enough away from the volunteers to have privacy. Ryan spoke soft enough that his voice wouldn't carry. "Are things serious between you?"

"God, I hope so."

Ryan snorted. "It just seems as if—" He stopped dead in his tracks.

Mack waited for him to continue, but Ryan seemed intent on the bottom of his teacup.

Mack hit his shoulder. "What?"

A gentle shrug. "You're not moving very fast."

Frustration welled up again, but this time Mack didn't succeed in holding it back. "I can't ask her to do anything until I can afford a place for us both, and until this month, every extra cent I've been making has been going to help my parents so they don't end up losing their home."

Ryan looked at him steadily for a moment. Then he nodded, a wry smile twisting his lips. "Being there for our parents—it's a great privilege. A burden at times, but…"

"No, I want to do it. They deserve all the help I can give them, and it wouldn't have been a big deal except it's meant holding my tongue when I would've liked to have spoken sooner."

"You'll get no harassment from me," Ryan told him. "I don't know what I would've done without my parents' help when Justina passed away. Anything I can do for them in the future— they won't even have to ask."

Finally sharing the truth let something inside Mack relax. "Don't tell anyone, please."

"Of course not." Ryan eyed him. "Does Brooke know?"

"She knows I've been sending them money, but I've never come right out and told her why. I didn't want her first introduction to them being the fact they got in financial trouble."

"Things are tight for everyone right now," Ryan pointed out. "I think she'd understand."

She would—but he still wanted to be able to do the next thing before he spoke.

Ryan rubbed his hands together. "So, on to the more important topic of what you're going to make for Brooke that absolutely screams how you feel about her."

"I think your idea of a picture is a good one. I think I've got one that would be perfect."

He opened up the photo app on his phone, pausing at the first image he hit.

He'd taken some shots of the photo album Brooke had found so he could use the images when he was adjusting the decorations. All of the rooftop cutouts were now LED compatible and low wattage, stored in the back of his truck for the opportunity to put them up wherever ended up being the most appropriate.

But in the mixed-up mess of pages with no organization at all, there were lots of pictures as well of a younger Gary Silver celebrating the holidays with Brooke's Gram and Grandpa. They were seated on old couches covered with throw cushions, Christmas cookies on a plate on the coffee table.

Legs crossed, one of Gary's feet was clearly visible. Slipper-clad.

Mack looked closer, sliding to another picture, and sure enough, they were there again, set after set of the infamous slippers that had begun this entire thing, and he realized he not only needed a present for Brooke, he needed one for Gary.

He was on his feet, still staring at the pictures, headed for his coat and shoes, when a soft laugh brought him back from his musings.

"Good to see a smile on your face again," Ryan said with a smirk.

It wasn't just a smile, it was knowing he'd been handed a

Christmas miracle and now knew *exactly* what needed to happen. Mack was out of the fire hall and driving through the wintry cold before he realized he was probably out of line visiting at this time of night.

But there were still lights on at the Heart Falls Seniors Lodge, and as he made his way in, the warm scent of supper lingered in the air combined with the sound of Christmas carols, and the tightness in his chest grew lighter.

A bolt of joy struck him at discovering Geraldine still sitting in the common area where the TV was set to the image of a flickering fireplace.

She looked at him and blinked. "Well, now, this is a surprise."

He dropped into the chair beside her. "I need your help."

7

One week before Christmas, and desperation was setting in. Something eventually had to work, even if Brooke had to go and capture a couple of Christmas elves and shake them until magical holiday goodness fell out of their pockets.

"You know, none of those ingredients are going to jump up and attack you." Mack slid in behind her, his strong body a wall at her back as his arms wrapped around and tugged her close.

"Never know. I've heard chocolate chips can be awfully menacing," she returned, twisting to face him and letting her annoyance slip away. "Sorry I'm being a grump. I'm very grateful you're letting me use the kitchen here at the fire hall to keep working on the disaster cookies."

"And the disaster muffins and the disaster cake." He caught her chin in his strong fingers and kissed her slow and steady until she wasn't really thinking about all the previous batches that had failed.

She wasn't really thinking about anything except his lips, his hands, his touch.

When he let her up for air, she clung to his shoulders to

keep from swaying. "Remind me again what we're doing tonight."

His wicked chuckle echoed through the room. "We're cooking."

"That's what I figured." She rubbed against him slowly, nibbling on her bottom lip as she stared at his mouth. "Getting all heated up sounds like a *great* idea."

Sadly, he stepped away, tapping her nose with his finger. "I'm on duty until Ryan relieves me, and there are two volunteers currently working on homework in the back room."

Brooke let out a long, hard-done-by sigh. "Fine, then I guess I'll have to torture kitchen implements instead of turning up the heat the way I really want to."

"Oh, to hell with good intentions." Mack caught her before she could turn away, sliding a hand against her lower back and pressing their bodies together.

The power behind his muscles was an edgy addiction. She wanted to run her hands all over him, to tease as she touched. To press her palms over the ridges of his abdomen and up his broad chest.

Or drop them lower to where thickness grew as he kissed her again. Demanding, challenging. Making it clear without words how much he wanted her.

She caught his collar and pulled back far enough to whisper. "I know. Me too."

Mack took a deep breath. "Brooke—"

The door opened behind them and they sprang apart. Brooke turned toward the recipes lined up on the table, distractedly trying to push aside the thoughts of her and Mack tangled together in a sexual haze.

Mack finished answering the question the volunteer had and then they were alone again.

He grinned sheepishly. "So. You want to do the cake, or the muffins first?"

They both got to work, carefully measuring into the mixing bowls. "What are we trying that's different this time?" Mack asked.

"Pastry flour instead of regular. And I double-checked at the grocery store for different varieties of baking powder and baking soda to see if anything there could make a difference in how much they rise. Something's wrong, but I *know* the recipe works. I remember the taste of them."

It wasn't how she wanted to spend the evening, but as they progressed to the point of putting what looked like delicious baked goods into the oven, Brooke had to admit it wasn't all bad.

She liked spending time with Mack, period. That sense of ease had returned as they moved around the kitchen in what was pretty much a dance.

It turned into an actual dance. As she closed the door of the oven and stood, Mack caught her by the fingers and tugged her into his arms. He had music playing on his phone, and he kept her up against him, close and intimate, as they swayed. His strong arms held her with absolute control.

Brooke rested her head on his chest and closed her eyes. "This is nice," she murmured.

"*Hmmmm.*"

He didn't stop, not even when the volunteers came into the room and offered a round of applause. In fact, Mack twirled her out and then back, which made their audience cheer a little louder.

"We're heading out," Charity said. "You need us to do anything before we leave?"

"Right. We could change the music, or sign you up for tango lessons," the other quipped.

Mack twirled Brooke expertly, dipping her over his arm and staring into her eyes. "I think we're okay."

The volunteers snickered but left with cheerful goodbyes.

"That wasn't very polite," Brooke teased as Mack continued to dance them around the kitchen.

"You're in my arms. I didn't need to interrupt that just to say goodbye."

There was something in his eyes. It was sensual, yet rich and full. Possessiveness, yet belonging. As if him not wanting to let go of her was perfect because not only did she want to be there, but if she got to choose, him being in *her* arms was the one thing she'd demand most as well.

He slowed their motion, barely moving now. Tight enough together that if they'd been skin to skin this would've been a dance of an entirely different nature.

"God, I want you." The words were whispered. His voice was deep and rasping as if escaping a barrier he hadn't wanted to breach. "I *need* you."

Her heart stuttered. "Mack."

"Let me make you feel good." It wasn't a demand. It was the request of a man dying of thirst.

"But—"

"*Brooke.*" A step above a growl. He spun her in his arms, once again looming over her. One hand caged her ribs, the other sliding over her belly to press her hips back against his.

His lips ghosted over her neck. Her ear. Teeth nipping at her earlobe before he sucked at the sensitive skin below.

She was melting. It didn't matter that the winter storm shaking the building was blowing hard enough to make the windows rattle. Ice crystals and freezing cold air stole in through whistling gaps.

His arms were a fiery furnace. His hand rose to collar her throat. Controlling yet gentle. Immobilizing her so when he slid his other hand under the waistline of her pants, she had nowhere to go.

"Open your legs for me," he whispered. "Let me touch you. Let me take what I need."

She was getting the better end of the deal, and as his fingers slid through her folds, Brooke couldn't stop the gasp of pleasure that escaped.

It was followed rapidly by another, his fingers strumming slowly as if he were playing her like a musical instrument. Teasing, rising to circle her clit then dropping before anything spectacular could happen.

She'd stepped with her feet apart, but he used his own leg to widen her stance even more. It left her slightly off balance as she stood spread-eagle, shaking in anticipation of his touch.

"There we go." He tucked his fingers deeper, sliding into her and leaving his palm pressed against the most sensitive part of her sex. "Now we're cooking."

Brooke closed her eyes as she placed her hands on his strong forearms, savouring the connection. Under her fingers, muscles flexed as the hand between her legs played. The other stayed steady and in control, his thumb caressing back and forth against her carotid artery.

Spiraling pleasure rose and she rocked against him. The motion was futile yet unstoppable, because she couldn't change a thing with her motion. She wasn't in charge, he was. Controlling the depth, controlling the pressure. Giving her exactly how much she needed for this to happen.

Drawing closer, his lips hovered at her ear. A sharp nip, and a spark flared, building in her core and edging outward as he picked up the pace just enough. Matching her harsh breathing, the warm air of his exhalations skimming over her cheek.

"I can't wait until I have you to myself. Somewhere private. Somewhere warm, so I can strip you down and then it won't be my fingers between your legs. It'll be my tongue, and after you've come, my cock. Pushing into you and filling you up."

"Mack—"

"I might even fuck you like this. Bend you over so I can bury myself deep then pull you up to hold both your breasts and lock you in place while I drive my cock into you."

"*Mack.*"

"Or I'll take you to the floor. Not on your back, but over me. Up on your knees far enough so you don't have to move and I can give you the ride of your life."

He teased his fingers out to catch hold of her clit, pinching in a tight circle before driving in and pressing the heel of his hand down hard.

She was gone. The spiral pleasure of heat that had been whirling inside was now an inferno, racing through her system and to the farthest edges of her limbs. She gasped for air, heart pounding, chest heaving. Body clamping down tight around his fingers as if she didn't want to let go.

It took a while to come to her full senses. That was when she realized that sometime during her orgasm, she'd dug her fingernails into his forearms. She swore as she let go, caressing the marks gently. "Sorry."

She got a kiss and a chuckle for her apology. "I like your claws."

The oven timer buzzed, and they both laughed.

"Well-timed," Brooke offered in a wavering voice, her strength still pooled somewhere around her toes.

Mack made sure she had her hands braced on the counter before he let go. "Give me a minute. Don't you try opening the oven or I'll spank your ass."

"Promises, promises."

He had his hands in the sink, washing up, when footsteps rang up the metal stairway. Brooke glanced over to discover Ryan bounding through the door with his usual enthusiasm.

"Hey, guys, something in here smells good."

Brooke picked up the oven mitts off the counter to keep her face hidden. "The smelling good part we've got down pat."

Mack stole the oven mitts from her, winking and sending

her cheeks flushing again. "Let me take care of this part. I'm good around hot things."

And even though a few minutes later it was clear that the muffins and the cake were less than successful, both crumbling into piles of inedible dust after being pried from the cooking pans, Brooke found it hard to be frustrated.

Spectacular orgasms had a way of making other disappointments vanish.

IT WAS NOT a message Mack had expected to receive. Yet there it was, plain and clear, hand-delivered by Ashton Stewart, the foreman at Silver Stone ranch and, as it turned out, one of Gary Silver's drinking and card buddies.

"Are you sure this is for me?" It was a stupid question, and the expression on Ashton's face said as much, but it seemed unbelievable.

"Not the kind of mistake I would make, delivering one man's mail to another." Ashton pointed at the envelope. "Gary gave that to me this morning when I stopped by. Said he couldn't leave the shop but needed to get in touch with you. Seems he doesn't have your phone number."

Mack read the message again. Nothing fancy, written in a broad pen on an old piece of newsprint. Probably the only thing Brooke's father had been able to find in the shop at the time.

We leave for the graveyard at four o'clock. Brooke will want you along.

"Okay." Mack glanced up to find the older man assessing him. "Graveyard visits. Anything you can tell me about that?"

"You asking what the protocol is in general, or something

specific?" Ashton adjusted his cowboy hat before slipping his fingers into his pockets.

"Both." Brooke hadn't said anything about a visit to her grandparents' gravesides being a part of their holiday traditions.

The older man thought for a moment before nodding firmly and looking Mack straight in the eye. "He's not quite sure what to think of you. Gary, I mean. But he thinks the world of his daughter, and he cared for his parents with a deep and powerful love. The fact he's invited you along means something."

Even though Gary had worded the invitation as something that *Brooke* would want, Mack considered for a moment, letting the truth sink in. A scary yet wonderful truth—her father knew he was important to Brooke. "Do I bring flowers or something?"

This time he got an awkward shrug. "Not a hundred percent sure, but flowers are usually appropriate. You should do what you think Brooke would like. Safer that way."

"Thank you. For bringing the note and for the advice."

"No problem. Interesting to see how this shakes out in the end." A slow smile spread across Ashton's face, deepening the laugh lines at the corners of his eyes. "Getting to the point in life where it's nice to have a few distractions, and you're turning out to be a fine one."

Meaning Gary had obviously been talking about Mack with his cronies. So be it—Mack had been wagging his tongue about Gary as well, at least with a couple friends he really trusted.

Still, some things couldn't be left without being poked.

Mack eyed the older man. "I think you need something to keep you occupied. Don't they keep you busy enough down at Silver Stone?"

"Lately? Not really. Enough new people running around that I have less to do on a daily basis. Besides, the goal of any good supervisor is to make sure they're replaceable."

"Maybe I should offer you a job here at the fire hall."

Mack had meant it as a joke, except the instant the words were out of his mouth, he remembered Alex's comment about needing new rotation leaders. Ashton Stewart was older yet still in prime condition, but more than that, he knew how to lead teams and get people to work hard.

"Let me know if you're serious about wanting a real distraction." Mack tucked the letter into his back pocket and straightened, looking Ashton over for a moment before continuing. "We could use you here at the fire station. And I don't mean to gossip about people's dating life."

Ashton looked intrigued but left without saying anything more.

Mack got things in order so he could take off on time, swinging by the florist to pick up two small bouquets. He pulled into the parking space at the Silver garage right as the *Open* sign was being flipped over to *Closed*.

He hurried to the service entrance, even the short time in the intense cold making his cheeks tingle in the warmth of the garage.

Brooke glanced up from where she was pulling on thick winter boots, shock in her eyes. "Hey. You're here."

He glanced around. Gary was at the far end of the shop, moving slowly with his back toward them. "You didn't tell me we had something on the agenda."

She scooted up and kissed him quickly before reaching for her coat and tugging it on. "I didn't know we had an agenda until breakfast when Dad told me he was closing down the shop so we could go to the gravesides."

Mack nodded. "He sent me a message. Invited me to come along."

Brooke paused in the middle of pulling her hair out of the back of her collar. "Oh."

"You didn't know?"

She shook her head, then pulled a heavy toque down over her ears. "It's a good thing. Isn't it?"

He slid closer, wrapping a hand around her waist and squeezing tight. "I'm glad I'm here."

Gary joined them, heavy boots already on and winter coat with its high collar turned up against the cold. He stared at Mack for a moment then dropped his chin decisively. "We should go in one vehicle. You drive."

Mack nearly fell over at the order, but he hurried to open the door for Brooke, swinging ahead of her to unlock his truck.

Gary waved off the offer of the front seat, climbing into the back of the crew cab. He paused when he spotted the bouquets resting on the center console.

It took a moment to get the truck started and the heaters blasting, then Mack turned to Brooke. "I picked these up for you. Seems like in most of those pictures you showed me, your grandma always had daisies and baby's breath around. Thought it would be appropriate." Mack met Gary's gaze in the rearview mirror. "I hope you don't mind."

Gary just kinda grumbled, but Brooke reached over and tangled her fingers in Mack's. "They're perfect. Thank you."

It was a quiet ride, the sun already sliding behind the mountains by the time they made it to the cemetery on the outskirts of town. The house beside the graveyard was lit up, a warm homey glow shining from the windows.

In the graveyard itself, teeny lights twinkled as if pixies were flitting amongst the stones and dancing in the bare branches of the conifer trees. Mack pulled into the parking space, thankful to see a path had been plowed into the cemetery's center.

Today had been the least blustery day in a while, but the wind still rumbled around them like icy fingers dragging at their clothes. Mack tucked Brooke closer to his side as they followed Gary down the slippery path toward the far corner where the land rose and fell like soft folds in a crumpled blanket, carrying on westward toward the foothills of the Rocky Mountains.

Gary came to a stop beside two small memorial stones that lay side by side. *Sharon and Emmanuel Silver.* Stark black against the pristine white, they were bordered by a small rosebush barren of leaves but glowing brightly with three hanging canning jars that seemed filled with firefly light.

Rose-coloured streaks shot out against the darkening sky. The wind whistled harder, and Brooke hid her face against Mack's chest, shivering slightly.

Gary turned back, his face pinched with the cold but resolution in his eyes. He met Mack's gaze. "I was totally out of line when I shouted at you two the other day. My dad would've busted my chops right then and there, and I know it. So, I'm sorry."

"It's okay, Dad." Brooke reached a gloved hand toward him, and he grabbed it and squeezed tight even as he shook his head.

"Nope. It's not okay. I was wrong. You don't remember, but your Grandpa got hurt one time setting up those decorations. Fell off the damn roof because he didn't wait for me to help. He was okay in the end, but it threw me. Seeing you two with ropes and ladders and those damn—" He took a deep breath then let it out carefully. "That's no excuse, but I just thought about how he got hurt out of the blue and the idea of that happening..."

His fears were understandable. It was also far more of a confession than Mack had expected to hear from the man.

Mack nodded. "Makes sense to me. The idea of anything happening to Brooke terrifies me too."

"You're not helping. I'm not made of crystal," Brooke deadpanned, obviously trying to break the tension. "But I appreciate what you're saying, Dad. We didn't mean to scare you."

Gary nodded. "I had kind of forgotten about those

decorations being there. I want to make it clear that I have no interest in seeing you on the roof of the shop putting them up —that's like a death sentence waiting to happen. But if there's somewhere else you want to put them, feel free."

The fire hall was out as an equally dangerous location, but an inkling of an idea had snuck in. "Maybe they'd be interested down at the Seniors Lodge."

"That's a great idea," Brooke said. She cuddled in closer as the wind picked up and fluttered her collar around her face.

Gary took a deep breath then motioned with his head toward the stones. "Why don't you put the flowers down, then we'll go get warmed up."

Brooke slipped the stems into the holders at the head of the graves. They all stood for a moment in silence, looking down at the bright yellow contrasting against the white. A moment of joy in the midst of utter nothing.

Then they were back in the truck and headed for the shop, but this time it was Gary who did the talking. Not as if he was spilling all the beans but sharing memories he couldn't contain.

"Dad and I made those decorations over a couple of years. They couldn't be made with new materials, not with my Dad's rules in place. No, everything was recycled and reused in those days, well before it was a catchphrase. It was a good lesson at times—that star was my first welding job. Put it together out of pieces from an old wagon I used to have. My favourite, now that I think of it."

In the rearview, Mack caught a glimpse of Gary looking thoughtful as he stared out at the growing darkness.

The older man continued. "I was proud of that star. I guess it will be good to see the lot of them up again and people enjoying the sight. Dad would have liked that."

The whole afternoon had been one incredible yet unexpected moment after another, but they'd hit the bad turn in the fairy tale. This was where Mack lost his footing.

Because out of all the decorations he and Brooke had rescued from the loft and everything he had revamped with new wiring to become a part of this year's Christmas celebration, there was obviously something missing.

There'd been candy canes, and trees, and a Santa Claus, and a whole lot of reindeer.

There hadn't been a single star.

8

Wooden floors underfoot echoed with the sounds of boots moving past the folding tables that had become impromptu workstations along the edge of the Rough Cut's dance floor. Music played in the background but not as loudly as on a typical evening when locals and visitors alike would pour through the doors into warmth and revelry.

This late afternoon event was still about Christmas cheer, though, and being with friends. Brooke glanced at the gathered crowd with a sense of glowing happiness.

And a hint of confusion.

"Why do they all look normal?" she asked Mack as he helped her off with her coat.

A snort of laughter and a quick grin flashed in her direction. "That's a terrible opening to give me."

"Just tell me when you spot it, Einstein," she teased back.

Because while it was obvious the assembly of Christmas hampers was going well, a growing stack of boxes lined up near the front door, the other portion of the event she'd been expecting seemed to be lacking for everyone except her and Mack.

A cheery *hello* hit her from two sides as Rose and Yvette both came into view.

Yvette had her arms wrapped around a box, but she paused to give Brooke a thorough examination before blinking hard. "You're looking very...bright and festive."

"What she looks like is a billboard in Times Square," Rose offered in return.

A soft curse escaped Mack's lips before he once again grinned. "You ladies know where Ryan is?"

"Don't tell him," Brooke warned before turning to Mack and adjusting the collar of the incredibly tacky sweater gracing his muscular body. "Remember, he's a good friend *and* it's the holiday season. You don't want to go and skin him or do anything remotely gory."

"Is Ryan the reason Mack currently looks like Mister Rogers on LSD?" Rose asked.

Yvette had added her box to the stack by the door and returned at that moment, gasping at Rose's comment. But it wasn't shock; it was amusement. "Number one, Mister Rogers would *never* stoop to using drugs. Number two, I kind of like the sweater. The fuzzy blue fruits on the tree look friendly."

"They're pears, and there's a partridge in there somewhere," Mack growled before shaking his head. "Okay, I won't kill him now. But I might save that option for later, if I get bored."

"What are you complaining about?" Brooke said sweetly as she linked her arm through his and followed the girls to where the assembly line began. "My ugly sweater has lights, and I still haven't figured out how to keep it from flashing SOS."

The man of the moment—Ryan—showed up, his expression welcoming, but nothing out of the usual. Nothing to show that he'd successfully pulled a fast one on them. "Glad you guys made it. Grab a box and run down the line. Add one of every can or package of dry goods, and at the end we'll add the perishable items."

"And at what point do I get to shove my favourite *turkey* in a box?" Mack asked, his voice a growl.

For one second, Ryan's lips twitched before he went back to looking smooth and debonair. "That would be the final perishable item."

"Jerk," Mack offered dryly.

"On the dry goods table. Teriyaki and peppered."

Ryan weaved back as Mack reached for him, then the two of them ended up scuffling good-naturedly as the women stepped closer together.

Rose watched the guys wrestle, one brow rising. "For grown-ups, they're doing rather fine imitations of preteens."

"I assume the ugly sweaters were Ryan's idea?" Yvette asked.

"He told us *everyone* would be wearing them. I twisted Mack's arm to make sure he participated." Brooke felt nothing but amusement at this point, the bright yellow sweater she'd found at the thrift shop and then woven LED lights all over making her feel more happy than foolish.

"You look cute." Yvette glanced at Mack who had given up trying to take Ryan to the floor and was now talking contentedly with the man as they stepped down the assembly line. "He, however, does look like an over-caffeinated Mister Rogers."

The three girls laughed softly then moved into position and got to work.

It didn't take long to finish putting together the food portion of the Christmas hampers, and they all took a break. They sprawled in chairs that had been brought in from the storage room, then cups of warm cider and bowls of home-baked snickerdoodles and whoopee pies were passed around the table.

"How do you decide what goes in a hamper?" Yvette asked Rose, who was the coordinator again this year.

"How do you decide what goes on the table on Christmas

Day?" Rose offered back. "A lot of it is tradition. Some of it is strictly for convenience. Mostly, though, it's not a great idea to pack ingredients that people don't know how to use at a time of year when trying new things would take more energy than they have."

Brooke mentally ran through the list of everything that had been put in these hampers for local families. "Are you saying a traditional Canadian Christmas in Heart Falls involves stuffing, a turkey, and green beans?"

"Pretty much, although I've been working with the newcomers' group. We try to add different ingredients when appropriate. In a couple of cases, instead of doing up a hamper, we were able to do a gift certificate so the families could get what they needed at the mercantile for their own traditions. Adding recipes is new as well."

"I saw the recipe part," Yvette said. "I got a basket from the welcome wagon when I moved in, and it included recipes for cabbage rolls and for paneer makhani."

"That sauce is fantastic with chickpeas as well," Rose shared.

Brooke applauded the changes, but she had to offer a wry confession. "I think it's absolutely awesome I can now learn to burn things from many different cultures."

Beside her, Mack was trying hard not to laugh.

"My best-ever Christmas dinner was arriving home from college to discover homemade mac & cheese in the fridge. My mom had made a huge pot of it for anyone who wanted a late-night snack. I got in so much trouble when I snuck in and devoured a bowlful about half an hour before the official family dinner." Yvette hummed happily. "Totally worth it."

"Food memories are the best." Mack said with a nod.

"Agreed, but I still think the best mac & cheese is KD." Alex got a round of cheers and jeers for that one, the cowboy having joined the group a little late.

"What's your favourite food memory?" Rose asked Ryan.

"Watching Talia take her first taste of ambrosia." His gaze slipped upward, and he stared at the heavy wooden beams decorating the ceiling. "Justina wasn't quite sure it was appropriate to serve to a little girl, but I insisted, and our friends backed me up."

Mack pressed a hand against his chest. "I forgive you for all your wrongdoings because you mentioned the food of the gods. Ambrosia is the *only* way to celebrate the holidays."

Ideas continued to be shared, laughter rising up often as the group spoke animatedly. Brooke paused to make a mental note, however.

She'd been trying to figure out exactly what to put on the table for *their* celebratory meal. Mack had promised to help her cook, thank goodness, and he'd already bought a turkey. It was currently somewhere at the fire hall, still frozen solid. He'd promised to take it out in enough time to thaw and be cooked up on Christmas Day.

The rest of the basics were doable. Potatoes, salads, pickles. She'd grab buns from Tansy's at the last minute possible.

But Brooke hadn't even thought about ambrosia, and it was one thing she knew she could make—it would be impossible to burn. And if it was one of Mack's favourites, it needed to be a part of their tradition.

He needed to be a part of her tradition.

Because Mack had stepped up in a big way over the past days. He'd been there for her *and* for her father, even though Gary didn't want to acknowledge it yet. No, Mack was most definitely a part of their family, and she was going to make sure he knew it.

MACK HELPED CARRY the boxes to the truck waiting outside. Between him, Ryan, Alex, and the other guys who had remained, it didn't take long. Then Ryan slipped away to help his staff get the pub ready to open, and Mack trailed after him.

His friend glanced down at the gaudy fabric covering Mack's chest but managed to keep a straight face. "You and Brooke sticking around?"

"I think so. I plan to get her out on the dance floor for a while."

Ryan moved quickly behind the bar, checking the taps and alcohol supply. "Thanks for being a good sport about the ugly-sweater thing. I couldn't resist."

"Can't believe I fell for it, but trust me," Mack said with enthusiastic evil promise, "some moment in the future, when you least expect it, ugly sweaters will be a part of your world."

They exchanged grins. Mack stepped forward to help Ryan exchange tanks on one of the pop dispensers.

"Can I bother you to take that to the back storage?" Ryan asked as one of his staff came forward with an urgent question.

Mack hefted the canister onto his shoulder. "No problem. Just tell Brooke where I went when she gets back so she doesn't think I abandoned her."

"Yeah, you don't want that. She might exchange you for a different model." Ryan was back in teasing mode. "Something with a little more get up and go."

Mack rolled his eyes. "Ass."

But Ryan wasn't listening, so Mack carried on into the back of the bar. He was familiar with the layout from his year in the community and hanging out with Ryan many a night.

He waved hello to the waitress who was getting out the float and setting up the till, then paced the hallway to the back of the building.

The storage room was orderly and neat, exactly how he expected it. Ryan was not the type to allow things to get into a mess. Mack carried his burden to the far left where a row of other canisters rested. It was entertaining to glance around at the masses of supplies on the shelves, and he turned slowly—

The room went dark.

"Dammit." He hadn't known the light was on a motion sensor. Mack waved an arm in the air, but nothing happened.

He was in the middle of pulling out his phone to use the flashlight when a low laugh reached his ears. A familiar laugh, followed by a familiar set of arms slipping around his waist from behind. Brooke's scent filled his senses.

"Don't be scared," she whispered. "I'm not going to hurt you."

"Hmm." His low hum deepened as her hands slipped lower. "That's good—that you're not here to hurt me. But you seem to have *some* kind of agenda."

Her palm was pressed firmly over his length, his interest in this twisted play becoming apparent. "I confess I'm attracted to your classy attire and your amazing body. I feel the need to take advantage of you," she said.

"My sweater turns you on?" Mack fought to keep from laughing because playing this semi-seriously was a hoot. "Well, who am I to deny a woman made wild by my purple pears? Ravish away."

Something hit his back. It took a second before he figured out it was Brooke's forehead and she was giggling uncontrollably.

He twisted and gathered her into his arms where she belonged. It didn't matter they stood in the dark in a storage room that smelled faintly like beer and peanuts.

They were together, and that made it perfect.

"You're a goof," she murmured, fingers sliding up his chest to tangle behind his neck. Brooke tugged him toward her until their mouths met. Her kiss was sweet, lips curled upward in a smile as they brushed slowly. Gently. So innocent it could have been their first.

Memories flashed. "You have no idea how much pain I was in that day we went to the archery range."

Air puffed past his cheek, an amused huff. "You're interrupting your ravishment to talk about target practice gone wrong?"

"I had never seen you like that before." He ignored her smart-ass comment and concentrated on his point. "You were this deadly warrior, all focus and power, and when you hit the bull's-eye on your second shot, I got a hard-on."

Her laughter rang clear and bright before she buried her face against his neck. "Stop." The words came out garbled. "I don't want anyone finding us yet."

"Just thought you needed to know. I was smitten from the first moment. And when you let me tug you against that hay bale and kiss you, I thought I'd gone to heaven. Tempting lips, body soft in all the right places, yet lethal and wild at the same time." He hummed as if he'd taken a bite of something delicious.

Brooke swayed, teasing their bodies together. "I like that memory. I like that you thought I was powerful."

"You still are." She could bring him to his knees if she chose.

With a brush of her hand down his chest, she was close to reducing him to incoherent rambling. She kissed his jaw, bit his lower lip. Her hand dropped over his groin and loosely contained his erection.

"I want something," she warned him.

"Okay." An instant response because he was smart.

Brooke chuckled. "The last couple times we fooled around, you've been very nice to me, but I haven't returned the favour. Let's do something about that."

"Trust me, getting you off makes my day. But no arguments

if you have different plans." He caught her chin in his fingers, turning her toward him so he could kiss her. It turned out a little rough as one hundred percent of his need came through.

He hadn't forgotten her comment about how sex between them always moved fast, but this didn't seem like the right place or time to make a change.

She pushed closer, fingers scrambling at his waistline. Lips still meshed, Mack claimed hold of her breast with one hand, shaping the fabric-covered mound with his palm.

It wasn't enough to feed the beast.

By the time she'd gotten his button and zipper undone, he'd slid his hand under her sweater, shoved away her bra and put his hand on her naked skin.

"God, you're wild today." Brooke breathed out the words as she wrapped her fingers around his cock.

His body rocked from the contact, the squeeze of her hand sending a pulse through him that threatened to break his control. "Play with me, angel. Whatever you want."

"You. Just you."

Him, broken and torn apart by driving lust. Or that's what it appeared she was aiming for as she dropped to her knees and sudden wet heat engulfed him.

Sensation threatened to overwhelm his senses. The darkness remained, turning her touch even more powerful. All-consuming. He could picture what she was doing, and the mental image of the intimate connection rocked him.

Brooke teased with her tongue, running it along the crown of his cock, focusing on the small spot she knew triggered the best sensations. The most powerful pleasure.

"Babe—I'm close." He whispered the words, stroking his fingers through her hair. Wishing he could see. Not for the erotic imagery but for the expression in her eyes. To savour the emotional connection between them. The physical connection was out of this world, and his release was rolling forward hard enough to make white spots appear in his vision.

He held back a shout, but something rumbled out of his chest. Not words. Nothing sensible, but a sound full of satisfaction and uncontrolled pleasure.

Flashing lights filled the storage room. Blink-blink-blink, flash-flash-flash, blink-blink-blink.

Mack's legs were unsteady as she rose from the floor, her sweater lighting up over and over again with comical timing. The smile on Brooke's face was clear in the resulting glow.

She cupped his face and let him lean on her briefly.

"SOS. Did I call for help?" he teased breathlessly.

"You were calling for something," she said.

Mack tucked her against him and hugged her tight. "Thank you."

"Any time."

His head still rang with the echo of his orgasm. Mack was thankful for Brooke's fingers in his as she led him back into the public part of the bar and onto the dance floor.

"I don't know if this is a good idea," he warned.

"You've got no sense of rhythm?" She was grinning like a Cheshire cat. Anyone looking carefully would know she'd just gotten her way in something big. She had that *look*. Contented woman, proud of her ability to reduce the average male to her willing servant.

It was true. If she asked, he'd do it. Anything for her.

God, he loved her.

Mack fought the urge to blurt it out by pulling her nearer. He wrapped his arms around her and tucked her tight against him. Dancing was mostly swaying with no attempt at making any fancy moves.

Brooke seemed content to follow his lead in this, as in so many circumstances before. She rested her head on his shoulder and they moved together like a well-oiled machine.

Mack wasn't sure if Ryan was being helpful and making sure there was a long run of slow, easy-to-waltz-to music, but he was grateful it was a long time before the pace picked up and he and Brooke had to slip farther apart.

Fingers locked together, fitting exactly right. The way their lives would when he finally found the moment.

Screw that, he would *make* the moment. He'd have to double-check, but maybe it was still possible to organize a last-minute getaway. He held his tongue until he could do some quick googling, but when her name was called and they turned to face Alex, he had a plan bubbling in his brain.

"Got a minute?" Alex winked at Brooke before leaning in to speak over the music. "I think I found something for you."

She frowned. "What did I lose?"

"The name of your song." He held up his phone then passed it over. Brooke clicked *play* then held it to her ear, covering her other ear to block the dance tune ringing off the walls.

A moment later, her eyes widened, and her smile flashed to brilliant. "That's *it*! Oh my God, you found it." She impulsively grabbed Alex and squeezed him tight.

Alex kept his hands in plain sight, but his grin when it met Mack's over Brooke's shoulder said how much he was enjoying his thank-you.

Mack resisted acting the caveman, but he was pleased when Brooke released his friend and instantly threw herself into Mack's arms. "We have the song!"

"That's awesome. Now you need to relearn how to sing it."

"Ugh." Brooke made a face, but she was snuggling under his arm as she faced Alex. "Great discovery, and I really appreciate it. You want to come serenade my dad on Christmas morning?"

Alex's denial was instant and firm. "I'm fine with karaoke, but not much else. The only real singer I know is Walker Stone. You could pop out to Silver Stone ranch and ask him."

"That's a good idea," Brooke nodded decisively. "Thanks again, Alex."

He offered her a wink, then gave Mack a salute before strolling toward a group of women and asking one to dance.

Brooke was back in Mack's arms, nudging him toward the dance floor, and he went willingly enough. Ideas were whirling, but he mostly felt a sense of satisfaction at having made the decision to set up the moment he could propose.

They were running short on time to coordinate the perfect old-fashioned Christmas. Desperately short, but somehow it seemed as if there was all the time in the world.

Because when he stared into Brooke's eyes, he saw eternity.

9

*B*uns and Roses held a smaller-than-usual crowd this Saturday morning, but Brooke had desperately needed a hot pick-me-up before starting the day at the shop. She had forty-five minutes before her dad would expect her to be ready and raring to go, with a full load of vehicles on the slate to get done before closing time.

Tansy lowered a plate with three delicate half-moon-shaped cookies and a steaming hot drink in front of Brooke. "Today's special. I call it a Winter Solstice. It's short and dark, yet brightness is just around the corner."

Brooke lifted the mug in the air. "You're lucky I trust you."

"You're lucky I love you," Tansy returned. "Try it."

A deep inhale over the mug told Brooke two things. "Coffee. Chocolate for sure, and...orange? That's the brightness, right?"

"Yup! And the short is because that's Ghirardelli chocolate, and anything bigger than a mini mug and you'd have consumed a full day's calories in one go." Tansy offered a wink. "See how I prevent problems so we don't have to diet come January?"

"You're a goddess." Brooke took a sip and velvet sex slid over her tongue. She all but moaned at her friend. "Or a demon. That's sinfully good."

The chair across the table from her pulled back, and she glanced up to stare into Mack's deep brown eyes. He winked, holding the chair for Sonora Fallen.

"Hey, Gramma." Tansy detoured to give her grandmother a hug. "A Winter Solstice for you as well?"

"Thank you, sweetie. And I'll have a plate of the German butter crescents as well." The older woman sat down and sighed happily.

"Sonora." Brooke took another deep inhale of the chocolatey goodness as Mack settled at the table as well. "Excuse me for being rude and drinking alone, but I'm not letting this get cold."

"I don't blame you." Sonora removed her toque and gloves and placed them in her coat pockets before shrugging out of the thick garment. Her silver and white hair was neatly pulled back into a braid that hung down the middle of her back. The laugh lines at the corner of her eyes deepened as she smiled at someone at another table before turning grey eyes toward Brooke. "Go ahead. Drink while it's hot."

Brooke took a sip of the glorious elixir.

Mack lifted a hand and rubbed the back of his neck. "Not that I want to overstep my boundaries, Sonora, but according to the news, there's a big storm brewing. Do you really think it was wise to walk into town?"

"I didn't walk the entire way," the older woman said primly. "I got a ride to the mercantile, then decided I wanted a hot drink."

The mercantile was over a mile away. The chance the sidewalks had been cleared between the buildings this early was slim. Brooke and Mack exchanged glances as Tansy interrupted them to bring in two more hot drinks and the requested cookies.

"I agree with Mack," Brooke said cautiously. "Why didn't you drive in yourself? Are you having car problems?"

Sonora stiffened, glancing over her shoulder to see where Tansy was before speaking quietly, as if she didn't want to be overheard. "I guess I can't lie about that since you're the one who will fix it. Yes, I had a slight problem backing up the other day. I think you and Gary will need to come get my truck with your trailer. The back bumper is in rough shape."

Fiercely independent, Sonora had more than enough family in town to give her a hand if she asked.

If she *asked*—that was the problem.

"I'll check with Dad and let you know when we can come grab the truck."

Brooke turned to face Mack and he leaned in close for a kiss. Without thinking, she caught him by the back of the neck and turned what he'd probably intended as a quick buss into something a lot more heated.

Whoops?

His eyes flashed with amusement as he pulled away. "Someone is looking for trouble today."

"With you? Always."

A soft chuckle carried to them. Sonora, innocently sipping her coffee as she stared intently toward the ceiling. "Wonderful decorations in here. Plenty of things to entertain a soul without having to play peekaboo."

Brooke eased away from Mack. Or tried to, only to find he had his hand curled around her waist and wasn't letting go. "Sorry about that," she offered the older woman.

Sonora gave her a sharp glance. "Never apologize for being in love."

A zing raced through Brooke along with an instant rush of heat. She didn't dare peek sideways at Mack to see how he was taking Sonora's proclamation.

Brooke wasn't about to deny it to herself. She had fallen one hundred percent for her soldier boy, and she was getting to the point where she didn't care who knew. The urge to play the "who, us?" game wasn't there either. She wasn't about to do that to Mack in front of his face.

To be honest, the fact he hadn't instantly denied it or made a joke to cover up any awkwardness only made her heart glow brighter. His fingers had tightened, but beyond that, he did nothing other than change the topic.

Mack focused on Sonora. "I was asking around, and it turns out you're the person we need to talk to. I'm trying to track down a decoration the United Church borrowed a few years ago. Your name came up in the conversation as someone who might know where it landed. Or who else we could talk to."

Sonora looked curious. "A Christmas decoration?"

Mack nodded. "A large metal star, about five feet in diameter. It would have had lights on it as well, and maybe a pole for suspending it above the rooftop."

He had been talking with his hands, animated and hopeful, and Brooke stared in fascination. She loved the way he spoke so earnestly and the way his eyes lit up when Sonora nodded immediately.

"I remember that." She frowned. "But I'd have assumed it would have gone back with the rest of the decorations. It's not in the storage shed outside the church?"

"No, ma'am. I looked."

He had? Brooke examined him closer, this man of hers who was surprising her with his earnest determination.

Sonora leaned back in her chair and turned thoughtful. "Well, that beats all. Although…I wonder." She pulled out her phone, but before she turned it on, she apologized. "Excuse me for being rude for a minute. I think I know who might have an idea where your star is."

A tight squeeze on her thigh and Brooke glanced at Mack who was trying to hide his smirk.

"She's adorable," Brooke whispered in his ear as she covertly watched Sonora type a message.

"*You're* amazing," Mack returned. "I don't have that much longer before I have to hit the hall, but I do have a question."

"Shoot."

"Can you run away with me tonight? I know it's last minute, and I know…"

Brooke's heart gave a leap. "Yes."

"…it might be hard to wiggle—" He stopped. A grin splitting his expression, he leaned closer and pressed their foreheads together. "You work until five. Can you be ready at five thirty? Overnight bag, swimsuit, comfy clothes. We'll toss our boots and emergency gear in the truck, just in case."

"Sounds fantastic."

They would have sat there grinning at each other until Mack was late for his shift and she'd missed her start time and gotten her dad off on the wrong foot to boot, except Sonora made a disgruntled announcement. "Well, that was a waste of time. He's not answering. I'll have to try again later, but I'll get back to you, Mack."

"Thanks, Sonora. I appreciate it." He kissed Brooke quickly then shot to his feet, money on the table to cover the cost of the food. "My treat, Sonora. And I'll see *you* later."

"Bye." Brooke watched him go, lazy satisfaction dripping through her veins as she admired his slow-paced stroll out the door.

"He is one fine man," Sonora said softly.

"He is at that," Brooke agreed.

Not even a minute later, the front door of the shop reopened, and another blast of cold air rolled in along with another fine gentleman, Ashton Stewart.

Brooke had enjoyed his sharp wit and kind gestures for many years, her father's friend a frequent visitor in their home. He was as good as family, in a way, which was why she'd found it equal parts amusing and horrifying to discover her girlfriends considered Ashton a very sexy, albeit older, specimen of the male cowboy species.

The girls' night out crew considered him a shining example of a man who'd aged well. Tansy had called him a juicy prime rib eye until Rose had pointed out that wasn't very PC.

Prime Angus beef hadn't made the cut, either.

But that morning, his square jawline and steel-grey eyes weren't showing his usual down-to-earth good humour. Now he was more along the lines of a bear that had been poked out of his den and was none too pleased with the poking.

He stomped across the floor to stop beside their table, glancing at Brooke and offering a quick chin nod before glaring at Sonora. "Are you out of your mind, woman?"

Sonora returned his stony stare before she deliberately glanced away and sipped her coffee. "Last time I checked, no."

Ashton dropped into the chair Mack had vacated. "When I offer to drive you to town, I expect you to stay put and let me drive you to all your destinations."

"I'm not a dog that you can order to sit and stay, Ashton. If you feel the need to practice your canine training, drop by the animal shelter." Her bright eyes narrowed. "Or maybe not. You'd just get them all riled up and then leave."

Ashton stiffened further.

Brooke enjoyed the final bit of her coffee and chocolate, watching the conversation with great amusement. She'd always suspected something brewed between these two, but it appeared the relationship had hit a stormy point.

Wind gusted hard enough against the front window to rattle the double-paned glass, snow slamming into the building seemingly out of nowhere.

In the short time she'd been in the coffee shop, the cold but clear day had vanished. The weather had turned. Another storm, this one unpredictable and violent.

"Wow. That's not looking very friendly." Brooke pushed back from the table to check outside. Whiteness blurred the buildings across the street.

"That's why I didn't want you wandering off." Ashton growled the words, but then he spoke more softly, his gaze on Sonora less of a laser beam as more concern showed through. "You know in this territory the storms sneak up quick. What if you'd still been walking when that hit?"

"I would have walked faster." But Sonora glanced past Ashton and out the window, and her flushed cheeks paled.

Ashton inhaled sharply and held it for a moment, as if fighting for control. He found it fast enough, turning to Brooke and mostly hiding the shake of his head and the slight eye roll of frustration. "I assume you're the one asking about the star?"

"Mack and I, yes. Do you know where it is?"

Ashton rubbed his jaw. "Maybe. I need to make a couple calls, but if I find it, I'll give you shout."

"Don't mention this to Dad," she asked. "We're trying to make it a surprise."

Ashton nodded then glanced between them. "You ladies go ahead and take your time. I'll drive you both where you're going when you're done."

Sonora pressed her lips together, but she didn't complain.

Brooke didn't either—the snowy weather wasn't going to be fun to walk through, and the sooner she got to the shop, the sooner she could throw a bag together to be ready for when Mack showed up.

~

WORK DRAGGED. There were only a few call-outs to distract him, even though Mack rode with the EMTs to their most common small-town emergency—home health calls.

The third time he helped pick up an elderly member of the

community off their snowy driveway, Mack moved from cursing the weather to wondering what made men challenge nature in stupid ways.

"You wait until the storm stops," Mack warned the older man who'd been trying to keep up with the snowfall and pushed himself to exhaustion. Thank goodness he hadn't had a heart attack. "If it's too deep for you to move, you've got neighbours with teenagers. Good chance to get them to build some muscle."

"Trying to build my muscle," the man complained good-naturedly, but he promised.

The storm howled like a wild creature. Only the people who hadn't heard the weather warnings were foolish enough to have headed to work. Most gave up by noon. By the middle of the afternoon, the people venturing out were stragglers closing up their empty shops, because four shopping days before Christmas or not, Heart Falls had turned into a ghost town.

The snow was now four feet deep in spots, the wind dropping to allow the piles to accumulate in peace. Mack didn't dare think about the hotel getaway he'd planned with Brooke. Thinking about it might jinx it, and he couldn't bear the thought of having to wait any longer.

He was going to propose before Christmas, no matter what. It *had* to happen. He needed to know she was his.

Five o'clock finally arrived. Mack already had his bag packed, and he made his way through the kitchen toward his truck and a night of freedom that could change his life forever.

"You look too happy," Alex teased. "I don't suppose you want to exchange shifts. I've got a back-to-back. You're welcome to replace me at six a.m."

"You need the beauty sleep more than me," Mack deadpanned.

Alex went serious. "God, let's hope it's a quiet night. This snow is going to make it hell to deal with any emergencies."

"Hopefully it started early enough most people stayed home." Mack said his farewells then hit the stairs. Bag in the truck, he checked to be sure he had an emergency kit just in case, then headed for Brooke's.

The snowplow rattled by, the man behind the wheel waving distractedly at Mack as he passed. Keeping a route between Main Street, the highway, and the hospital clear was vital. Mack didn't envy the endless task it was going to be under these conditions.

It did, however, make getting to the auto shop possible. Mack was probably not thinking straight—okay, he totally wasn't thinking straight—because what he should do was call and cancel, but damn if he could bring himself to do that.

He had winter tires, a high clearance vehicle, and he knew the roads around the area like the back of his hand. Over a year of driving to every corner meant he was comfortable going anywhere.

As he pulled into the space in front of the shop, the tires groaned, crunching on the heavy snowpack. He left the vehicle running, stepping into the shop and finding absolute quiet.

Gary and Brooke ran the shop by themselves with just a few hired hands during the busy season, so it wasn't unexpected. It was eerie, though. The absolute stillness meant each of Mack's footsteps echoed loudly as he walked toward the interior door leading upstairs.

Brooke burst out of the door, a duffle bag in her hand. Her cheeks were rosy, her brown hair covered with a bright red toque. "I'm ready."

He caught her as she threw herself forward enthusiastically. "You look ready."

She wrinkled her nose. "It's not nice out. I don't want to cancel, but you have to decide if you're comfortable driving."

"We'll be okay. We're not going far." And truthfully, that was the only reason he was proceeding. No matter how important this was, he wouldn't risk Brooke's safety.

Her smile doubled in size. "Then let's go."

Mack threw her duffle in the back of the crew cab, then helped her into the passenger seat. "Buckle up on this side, just to be safe."

"Yes, cap."

By the time he'd rushed around and seated himself, Brooke's seatbelt was tight and she had music playing. He backed out slowly, the accumulation still coming down but the snowfall lighter.

"The storm might be passing," Brooke said as he aimed the nose of the truck toward the main road. "Maybe the weathermen were wrong and it's not going to be anything huge. I mean, that was a lot of precipitation in a short time, but less than twelve hours of snow isn't the storm of the decade."

"Could be they were wrong." Mack eased the wheel to the right in preparation for pulling out of the parking lot. "Who knows with the—"

A sharp flash went off in the distance. White, then red and yellow, with a billowing cloud of black roiling upward from where they'd been headed. A loud bang hit the truck a moment later as the sound of the explosion caught up, and horror shot through him.

"Oh my God, is that the Exxon on the highway?" Brooke leaned forward in her seat.

Mack was about to answer when his phone went off. Simultaneously, the alarms in his truck sounded, the ones linked to the fire hall switchboard.

He glanced at Brooke, whose face was white with alarm. "I have to answer."

Mack jammed the stick into park and opened his phone. He listened to the report from 911 with horror.

It was bad. "Someone missed a turn and went through the

front window at the gas station a few minutes ago. It must have triggered a chain reaction. The car didn't explode, but they suspect a gas line ruptured."

"I hope there weren't a lot of people in the place." Brooke's eyes were wide. "The restaurant…"

The familiar adrenaline rush Mack felt in these circumstances was building. While he might have the evening off, this wasn't the time to run out on his teammates. "I'm sorry, I have to go."

He wanted to reassure Brooke, but she had already undone her seat belt and leaned in close so she could kiss him fiercely. She was out of the truck an instant later.

"Stay safe." It was an order, her gaze direct and intense as she held the truck door open. "I know they need you."

He waited until she was safely inside before shoving the truck into gear and hitting the gas. Hurrying toward the fire hall where he could make the biggest difference. Help the most people.

His heart, though, was back at the shop, climbing the stairs and probably already googling to see what had happened. Her thoughts would be on him and his safety.

Mack focused. It wasn't what he'd been hoping for, but if he wanted to get back so the next time he saw Brooke he could follow through on his plans, he had to get his head in the game.

Even as he drove steadily toward the danger, he wanted to be sure to come home. Getting hurt now was the last thing he wanted.

Brooke, forever, was worth being careful for.

10

The morning dawned very differently than Brooke had hoped. Instead of being curled up in bed with Mack after a soul-satisfying evening, she was at home listening to her dad bang around in the kitchen.

She stared at the ceiling and attempted to recalibrate her day by counting her blessings.

First, Mack had sent an email at five a.m. to let her know he was safe and back at the fire hall and to warn her he'd probably spend a lot of the day sleeping but he'd be in touch as soon as he was vertical. As a big-picture thing, that was pretty much at the top of her list.

She didn't blame him for their evening being cancelled. Being available in an emergency was part of his job, and from what she had discovered in her searching, the fire had been a bad one. Thankfully, with the storm there hadn't been a lot of people in the building, but there had been injuries.

What a horrifying twist to pre-Christmas preparations. Yet there'd been no fatalities reported and being alive was a good alternative.

Also on the good side—the storm had stopped. The rough

weather had fooled them all by being intense but brief, and while there were huge piles of snow everywhere, the sun shone with an almost violent intensity and the temperature was nearly above freezing instead of the chilling cold they'd had a few days ago.

She slipped into the kitchen and snuck up on her father. "Hey, Pops. You make enough coffee for me?"

"Never," he teased. "Besides, it's from the coffeemaker, not that fancy stuff your friend Tansy makes. I don't think you should even try a cup."

She poked him in the ribs. He snorted, moving out of her way so she could reach the cups.

Having her dad so visibly content made something in her happy as well. "You're perky this morning," she drawled. "How many cups of this terrible brew have you already consumed?"

"Only two." He refilled his cup then held up the milk box that was source of his glee. "I love eggnog season."

"Enjoy it while you can," she said, settling at the table and considering what she could do to pass the time. Sunday meant she had the day off, but there was no guarantee Mack would be ready to do anything with her.

Her dad flipped through the pages of his appointment calendar. "I might have spoken too soon when I said work was slowing down. We've scheduled time off for the holidays, but tomorrow we're booked solid."

"That's good," Brooke said. "Means I can afford to go back to the store and buy a box of Peek Freans to leave with Santa's milk."

Dad chuckled. "Get the ones with the strawberry middles. I hear he likes those."

She joined his laughter, but a trickle of sadness slid in with her amusement. Stocking up on store-bought cookies was on her "give up already, we're desperate" list, and she was rapidly closing in on that date. She still hadn't successfully managed a batch of cookies from Gram's recipe that tasted anything like the original.

Scratch that. She hadn't yet baked a cookie from the recipe that was *edible*, forget matching the perfect old-fashioned flavor. Their holiday baking was going to be reduced to fruit cremes and shortcake out of a box.

She forced a smile to her lips and made them breakfast.

When Mack didn't return her message—he was probably still sleeping—Brooke made the decision to get a few things off her to-do list.

"You think the roads are safe enough to go for a drive?" she asked after cleaning up her plate.

Dad nodded. "Guess the storm didn't want to be one for the record books. Snowplow already cleared everything in town, and Ashton phoned to say they weren't buried too badly at Silver Stone."

"Good, because I'm thinking about heading out there, as well as a couple other places." Happiness swelled. "I need to drop off presents for my girlfriends, because I didn't have them ready for our last get-together."

"You'll be fine." Her dad paused. "You hear from that guy of yours, yet?"

"Other than his message early this morning saying he was safe, nothing." She didn't have the bandwidth to tease about her father avoiding Mack's name.

Dad grunted, then paced away, muttering to himself. "Floor's cold. Got to get thicker socks on. See you later."

She was already turning to get ready herself when he caught her off guard and spoke again.

"Maybe you should drop by to check on him."

"Him, who?"

"Your guy." Her dad had paused in the doorway to his side of the apartment, his expression thoughtful as he met her gaze. "Must have been a rough night. He'd probably like to see you."

Wow. Brooke was speechless.

Good thing her father didn't seem to be waiting for a response. He'd said his piece then turned and walked away, leaving her dumbfounded.

Well, that was...

Wow.

Something warm and hopeful rested behind her breast bone. Like an oven turned on low to heat up, a glow started inside.

The happy sensation only grew as she made her way around town, dropping off presents for Tansy and Rose, then heading to Silver Stone because she could leave four presents there and know they'd get to their targets.

She'd known Kelli Stone back when she was Kelli James, and it would have made the most sense to head over to her home on the far side of Big Sky Lake, but the collection of vehicles outside the main Silver Stone ranch house told a story all in themselves.

Brooke laughed, identifying the fleet of trucks from the many times she'd worked on them. She parked in an open space and pulled out her phone to message her friend.

Brooke: *You guys having your family gathering a few days early?*

Kelli: *Are you one of Santa's elves who knows all and sees all?*

Brooke: *no, I am not one of those creepy Elf-on-a-Shelf things. I am outside and about to suggest you guys invest in shares of asphalt. Your parking lot is going to rival a Walmart if you're not careful.*

Kelli: *lol. Come in. We're not doing anything officially family-like right now other than herding kids. Bonus, there's leftover bacon from breakfast.*

Brooke: *just for a minute. I bring gifts.*

Kelli: *you definitely deserve bacon.*

Brooke grabbed her oversized bag from the passenger seat and headed up the cleared sidewalk to the back door.

Silver Stone was set in a beautiful part of the foothills, and with the thick blanket of snow that had fallen, everything was pristine and Christmas-card beautiful.

Inside the house was warm chaos. Children's laughter rang and the scent of maple syrup and bacon hung heavy on the air. Brooke glanced toward the living room and spotted most of the Stone family lounging on the couches and easy chairs in front of the fire. Other than a couple of Christmas cards on the mantle, there was no sign of a Christmas tree or any other decorations.

"Hey." Her friend Kelli enveloped her in a huge hug before pulling back and turning serious. "Mack okay? We heard about the fire."

"He's good," Brooke said.

Kelli breathed out heavily. "Good. I was worried when Ashton said gossip at the coffee shop was a couple of the firefighters had been injured."

Brooke fought to keep from stiffening. Was Mack really okay? He would have told her if he wasn't.

Wouldn't he?

She twisted her lips into a smile and pushed forward. "I'm not staying for long. I've got presents..." She slowed and considered her words carefully as Emma Stone, all of nine years old, moved into earshot. "Some from me and some that Santa dropped off for safe keeping."

Kelli's eyes flashed with amusement. "We can take care of those."

Tamara Stone ambled up, eight-month-old Tyler resting on

her hip. "Haven't seen you for a bit," she said, leaning in to offer a one-armed hug. "I have a body ornament today. Kiddo is running a teeny bit of a temperature, so he's in hyper-cuddle mode."

"Poor kid." Brooke ruffled the hair on the top of his head before she pulled the biggest present out of the bag on the table and offered it to Tamara. "For you. Purchased according to our chick-code."

"White elephant? Useful, but no longer used?"

"Open it and see," Brooke ordered.

Tyler chose that moment to thrust his arms toward Brooke. Which was how she ended up with a slightly sweaty infant cradled in her arms as Tamara hurried to deal with the newspaper-wrapped boxlike object.

"Get out." Delight rang in Tamara's voice. She turned to Brooke and deliberately pushed up her glasses. Pale green today, they matched the colour of her sweater. "This is a display rack for eyewear."

"They were getting rid of the old one at the optometrists, and I was in the right place at the right time." Brooke adjusted Tyler a little closer. "I hope there's room for all of your collection."

"I love it. Thank you." Tamara hugged her tight, and in the whirl of activity that followed, Brooke found herself moving with the flow, still in possession of little Tyler.

He didn't seem to mind. His big eyes examined her carefully, but then he laid his head on her chest and relaxed, watching the activity in the room with lazy interest.

Brooke found a spot to one side of the couch, content to watch the action herself as Tyler slipped into sleep. Conversations were happening and a puzzle was being worked on in the corner of the room. Kelli and Tamara had returned to the kitchen to join Lisa Coleman who was vigorously mixing something in a bowl, her little terrier wandering underfoot protectively.

There were a couple of adults playing cards, and another playing Jenga with the oldest of the children, Sasha.

A set of children rushed past, and then another, followed by their youngest uncle who was roaring like a bear. Music played, voices carried in small pockets, and they all seemed happy to have her there but none of them were worried they had to entertain her.

It was...family. Not like what she'd had growing up, but she felt comfortable in it, nevertheless. Yet as Tyler made a little cooing noise, wiggling tighter against her, something in Brooke's heart ached.

She ended up sticking around for the morning, basking in the joy even as a hint of worry continued to nudge her. She said goodbye right before lunch, begging off joining them for the meal.

Brooke was just about at her truck when a waving hand caught her attention. "Yvette?"

Her new friend rushed to a stop, breathing heavily after her sprint from the barns. "If you're headed to town, can I get a ride?"

"No problem."

Out on the highway, Yvette explained, "I drove out with Josiah to deal with a task. This way he gets to stick around instead of driving me home then having to turn around and come all the way back."

"Makes sense. You want your apartment?"

"No, the seniors lodge, please. I promised Mormor and Morfar I'd stop in."

Which wasn't a bad idea.

"Can I join you?" Brooke asked. Mack still hadn't texted her, and she needed a distraction before she ended up racing over and demanding to inspect him from head to toe. "And what about lunch first, my treat?"

Yvette agreed and they headed to Buns and Roses for a quick meal. Relaxing and entertaining at the same time, because Yvette was keen to learn everything she could about Heart Falls. The conversation flowed smoothly, comfortably.

It reminded Brooke a lot of the early days of being with Mack. That had been easy, too. As if they belonged together and slid into a comfortable routine without even trying.

Rich friendships like that weren't a thing to be taken for granted.

The lodge was fully decorated on the inside, but Brooke smiled at the thought of Mack's mission for the following day. They'd offered the restored rooftop decorations to the Lodge, with free labour to assemble and remove them once the holidays were over, and the manager had been delighted. Mack and Ryan had promised to put them up Monday.

If he was up for it. If he hadn't been hurt and was even now lying in bed suffering...

Brooke caught herself frowning. She made sure to hide her worry as she and Yvette headed toward Geraldine and Floyd's room.

They didn't even have to travel that far. Floyd wasn't around, but Geraldine was sitting in the middle of the common room, knitting needles moving slowly but without ceasing.

She glanced up as they sat. "Well, this is a nice surprise."

"I'm done with work for the day," Yvette said, pressing a kiss to her grandmother's cheek. "Where's Morfar?"

"Bothering the cooks. He's looking for cookies again." Geraldine put her hands at rest on top of her knitting. "When he forgets a thing, he forgets it pretty thoroughly, but for some reason he's stuck like glue on this one request."

"Toffee almond sandies are important," Yvette said seriously.

Geraldine motioned her agreement as if they were of the utmost importance. Then she turned to Brooke. "How's your young man doing working on his—" Her eyes widened, and she coughed a few times, picking up her knitting and distractedly trying to change the topic. "I hear they plan to have ham *and* turkey on Christmas Day."

Brooke eyed her with suspicion but let whatever she was keeping secret slide. "It sounds like a multitude of blessings."

"The food is usually good, but they work extra hard during the holidays," Geraldine shared. "And there'll be church service for those who like that and presents for everyone. My favourite part is the singing, although I'm not nearly as good as Floyd. He's the one with the voice of an angel."

"Singing was something we did a lot of when I was growing up," Yvette said.

Brooke leaned in closer. "Definitely not one of my skills, although I do have my favourite songs that my gram taught us."

Inspiration struck, and she pulled her phone out and flipped to the song she'd bookmarked on YouTube. She turned it on, and the most amazing thing happened.

Yvette's eyes brightened and she began to hum along.

Geraldine? She began to sing, her voice slightly wavering, but a rosy smile on her face as she accompanied the soloist.

When the song ended Brooke felt as if she should give a standing ovation. "That was beautiful, Mrs. Wright."

The older woman tilted her head in acknowledgement. "That is a part of Christmas I enjoy. You'll have to play that for Floyd. It would make his day."

Ideas bubbled, but Brooke held her tongue until she had a chance to run it past Mack. But this much she could promise. "I will make sure he gets a chance to hear it."

They continued to visit for a while longer. Brooke checked her phone numerous times, but there were still no messages from Mack. Three o'clock came and she couldn't take it any longer. She said her goodbyes then slipped away and headed to the fire hall.

The scent of smoke was stronger than usual, and her feet moved faster without trying, rushing up the stairs into the dining hall.

Brad was there, talking seriously with two members of the team. He didn't get up from the table, his words soft, his focus intent. She didn't want to interrupt him, but she needed to know—

As if he'd read her mind, Brad paused and made eye contact. He smiled, then tipped his head toward the bunk area. "He said he was headed back to get some more rest."

Brooke kept her pace short of a run but made it to Mack's room in double-quick time.

He wasn't there.

The sheets were rumpled, and the lights low, and she was about to head out on a search mission when a warm body pressed against her from behind, herding her into the room so he could close the door and envelop her in a tight hug.

She squeezed him back as well before letting go just enough to take a glance upward— "*Mack*."

His lips curled. "Merely a flesh wound."

"You said you weren't hurt." Brooke lifted a hand to his head where a white bandage shone starkly against his tanned skin. She hesitated before making contact, her stomach clenching with worry.

"Hey." He caught her fingers in his and kissed her knuckles. "It's okay, babe. Really. It was stupid—I had my helmet off while taking a breather, and I moved too close to a bare wall. I'm more embarrassed than hurt. Just took off some skin, but head wounds bleed more impressively than anywhere else. That's the only reason for this."

He tapped the cotton padding.

Brooke's heart was still racing. She looked him over rapidly, checking for any other outward sign he was keeping anything from her. "You should have told me."

"I was going to. As soon as I saw you in person, so you couldn't start envisioning all kinds of worst-case scenarios." He wrapped his arms around her and kissed her quickly. "Which is now. Hey, babe, I didn't duck fast enough, but my brains are still in the right spot. It's all okay."

It was tough to stay uptight when he was cuddling her close, but there was still a knot inside she hadn't felt before. "There's this thing called a phone…"

"Great inventions. They simply need to make one that's Mack-proof." He tilted her head back so he could look into her eyes. "If cooking is your kryptonite, phones are mine. It got crushed when I was rushing to make the transition to the fire truck last night."

That's why he'd emailed. Probably from the fire hall desktop.

"And I did phone, but it went to your voice mail. Honestly, I pretty much slept until about an hour ago." He led her toward the mattress since that was the only place to sit other than in the single chair in the corner. "But I'm glad you're here now."

Mack settled on the bed and tugged her into his lap. He refused to let her go anywhere except up against him.

Brooke leaned into him in much the same way Tyler had done to her earlier in the day. She brushed her hand slowly over Mack's cheek, then down the front of his sinfully soft T-shirt. His breathing was smooth and steady, but there was tightness in his torso that said he wasn't completely in the here and now.

"You want to talk about it?"

He hesitated, then nodded. "It was bad. Things went up hard, and they went up fast. The kid in the car was barely nineteen. He's alive, and by some freak circumstance, he's broken, not burned. Just lost control on the corner and couldn't stop."

"They have concrete barriers in front of the windows," Brooke whispered. "They're supposed to stop cars from leaving the parking lot."

"They work when the snow isn't twice their height and creating a dandy ramp. It was a fluke. Everything was in the wrong spot at the wrong moment. Someone was in the middle of moving a welder's tank, and they understandably freaked out when they saw a car flying toward them. The connections broke and compression failed." Mack leaned onto the bed and pulled her lengthwise against him. Far enough away that he could stare into her face.

He stroked her hair back behind her ear, his gaze softening.

"We got all the occupants out. The team did great and Fort MacLeod sent an ambulance, so that was completed as quickly as possible. Which was slow as molasses because of the snow. But the fire? It was too hot to put out."

Brooke pressed her hands to his chest and stroked. Petting him and willing him to share what he needed. Wanting to make this better.

His expression lightened. "Truth is, other than the cold and the snow and the fire and the firecracker display that went off at about three a.m., it was pretty routine."

"*Mack.*"

He kissed her, leaning in and taking what he wanted. His hard body slid along hers and then over for the briefest of moments. Brooke closed her eyes and breathed him in. Accepted his urgency and his need.

Then he was gone, rolling off the bed and glancing back with a sheepish grin. "Change my bandage? I just had a shower and it's wet."

He brought the supplies to the mattress and she worked carefully. Soothing the edges of the harsh red mark with cream and offering sympathetic murmurs at the rising bruise. "You don't have a concussion?"

"My head's too hard." She poked his shoulder gently in rebuke, and he grinned. "Hey, the EMT said that, not me. But it's true. Just a gash."

Once she was done, he sat back on the bed. "I slept most of the day, but I'm ready to crash again."

"Want some company?"

His expression lit up, then drooped. "It's a no fun zone tonight. I'm not—"

Brooke pressed her fingers to his lips and guided him back to the mattress. "We don't get many chances to cuddle. I'm not going to complain."

Mack hummed his approval, then broke off into a huge yawn. "Sorry."

She laughed softly. "Get comfy."

"You too." His words were slowing, his exhaustion showing.

She kicked off her shoes, jeans and top, stealing his T-shirt the instant it dropped from his torso. His head resting on his firm biceps, he watched her with heavy-lidded eyes.

Brooke lay beside him and he pulled her leg over his, his hand resting on her hip. She tugged the quilt over them, and they quieted, face to face in the near dark.

Small sounds carried from other parts of the fire hall but here it was only them.

His lashes rose and fell. Breathing slowing. "I'm glad you're here," he whispered.

"Me too."

He fell asleep between one breath and the next, the grip on her hip softening but still possessive.

It was the middle of the afternoon, so Brooke was nowhere near ready to sleep. But it was the ache in her heart that sent her mind whirling. While she'd done nothing wrong, something was still wrong, big time.

"I wish I'd been there for you this morning." She whispered the confession.

Yes, he'd told her he'd slept most of the day, but this stupid existence where being apart from each other was the norm—it meant she hadn't known. Hadn't known that he was hurt, hadn't been there to see he was hurting inside.

She didn't regret her amazing day because in it she'd caught glimpses of what she wanted in her world. Bits of a future out there that could be *theirs*, with family and friends and laughter and love.

This place they were in was no-man's-land—it wasn't right, and she'd had enough of pretending it was. That was the part that was broken and needed to be fixed.

"I love you." Another whisper.

What existed between them was a comfortable thing that had grown so big it was threatening to explode her heart from the inside out. She was going to make this right. They needed to be together for real.

Brooke laid in the quiet and watched her heart sleep.

11

They had an audience.

Not only that, but with the group of seniors who had braved the cold on this Monday afternoon, Mack and Ryan had at least a dozen supervisors and suggestion-makers.

It was entertaining.

The group stood in their bundled-up coats, a tight pack of elderly eyes staring up with great interest.

"More to the left," one of them shouted at the same time another suggested farther to the right.

Ryan's unwavering calm was showing signs of wear, but Mack was having a blast. Putting the decorations up at the Heart Falls Seniors Lodge was turning out to be a huge success, not just in terms of using the bits of memory from the Silver family, but in making a lot of other people happy.

When he'd woken that morning, he hadn't been sure this was going to happen. He and Ryan had organized the decorating detail a few days earlier, but either the storm or the fire might have messed up their plans.

But the storm had passed, and while it was still cold, the skies had gone bright blue again. Mack was caught up on his sleep, although he was slightly embarrassed he'd had Brooke in his bed and barely remembered her being there.

Other than the sense of peace she'd brought—that part he remembered just fine. And the worry in her eyes at his stupid head bump. He'd already switched to a smaller piece of gauze, just enough to keep the knit surface of his toque off the scrape.

He and Ryan had shoveled clear paths on the roof to make firm bases for the wooden frames, but in some ways the snow was a help now instead of a hindrance.

Ryan swayed to one side, dodging a snowball one of the more active seniors had lobbed in his direction. "Hey. None of that," he ordered. "We're hard-working volunteers, not practice targets."

"There's this thing called multitasking. You can be both at the same time," the mischief-maker shouted back, but he brushed the snow off his gloves and went back to flirting with the woman in the bright green coat next to him.

Lighthearted amusement was a good therapy for the heaviness Mack felt in his heart after the fire. He didn't usually get morose when it came to his job. Sometimes bad things happened, and he moved on and dealt with it.

Missing the planned time away with Brooke made it harder this go-round.

The second part of what was bothering him involved the downfall of working in a small town. It had been the same when he'd been deployed as a firefighter with the Air Force. That small town and community feeling meant he knew who had been hurt by the disaster. They were all connected and not nameless faces in a crowd.

Mack had met the family who owned the gas station. To know that in one fell swoop they had lost everything—it was a chilling reminder of how quickly life could change.

Yet looking down at the faces of the people below him who were enjoying the very tame entertainment of two grown men propping a Santa figure on their roof, Mack was also reminded small joys were huge.

It didn't take a lot of time to shove a person from contentment to sorrow. When everything could be gone in an instant, living life to the fullest when given the chance was the most important lesson he needed to remember.

Had he been going about this all wrong? He'd been hoping to make his proposal flashy and memorable, but was that what really mattered?

Mack had finally reached the point where he could afford to say something about how he felt and be able to do the next thing about it. Hell, he'd come close to blurting it out yesterday when she'd been there in his bed, soft and giving. Worry in her eyes and yet pride there as well.

He loved her so much. That was what mattered, wasn't it?

Icy coldness shattered against the side of his neck, shards of a snowball breaking apart and crumbling inside his collar. Mack cursed softly then glanced over at Ryan.

With his back turned and the unsteady footing, the other man was too far away to be the culprit.

Mack checked the crowd of seniors who were still foolhardy enough to be hanging around outside. They were now huddled close in a dandy imitation of a pack of wolves, keeping each other warm. His assailant wasn't any of them unless they were spry enough to have leapt back into the heap without knocking the rest of them over like dominoes.

He casually reached down and scooped up snow, forming it into a perfect ball.

If the answer wasn't A, then logically it had to be B...

He was about to fling his missile at Ryan's head when movement revealed a sheepskin jean jacket inching past the edge of the hedge between the lodge and the house to the west.

Suddenly, Ashton Stewart stepped forward, pure innocence in his expression. He whistled casually as he paced the sidewalk before glancing up as if surprised to find Mack on the roof. "Well, hello."

Mack raised a brow. "Fancy meeting you here. Out for a stroll?"

"Getting some exercise, yes." Ashton waved a greeting at Ryan before turning back to Mack. "Have some news for you about that item you're looking for. If you drop the ammunition you're holding, I'll tell you about it."

Instead, Mack tossed the snowball skyward, catching it in his hand a few times as he offered Ashton a steely glare. "Maybe you'll tell me what you know so I don't retaliate. I do have the upper hand."

Snowballs hit him simultaneously on the side of his head, his shoulder, and his back, and he twisted to see the seniors had taken advantage of his lack of concentration to mount their own attack. He also spotted the reason they were throwing like baseball heroes in spite of their age.

"Hey. Are those dog-ball throwers? Where's the sport in that?" Mack complained with amusement.

"When you're eighty, you get to use any advantage you want," was the response.

Not much Mack could say to argue with that.

Ryan grinned as he tipped his head to the side and motioned for Mack to join him. "We're pretty much done. Let's get off this roof so we present a smaller target."

They met on the sidewalk beside Mack's truck.

"I'm going to head out," Ryan said. "Talia will be ready to be picked up, and we're driving out to Black Diamond to my parents'. I'll be back in town for my Christmas Day shift."

Mack shook his hand firmly. "Happy holidays, and thanks for your help here. I'll be in touch."

His friend stepped away.

Ashton leaned back on the side of the truck, watching Ryan

head down the street with a firm stride. "He's been a good addition to Heart Falls," the older man said.

It was an entertaining thought. "I've been here less time than Ryan. You make a decision on me yet?"

Ashton chuckled. "I told you before, you're entertaining. And you present good puzzles—I had a hell of a time tracking down Gary's star."

"So, you figured out who's got it stashed away?"

A quick nod. "Only it's not the easiest place in the county to get to."

He told Mack the general area, and while the location wasn't far from town, Ashton was right. The access roads were all on the other side of the property to avoid running across the river, making a short trip into a much longer one.

Mack took a considering glance at the sky. Blue overhead, with clouds building over the mountains. "You think the weather will hold for long enough so I can make a run out there to grab it?"

The older man considered, eyeing the horizon with a knowledgeable gaze. "Usually when it starts building like that you've got at least a day before things shift. But we're pretty out of sorts here with how the recent storm turned everything upside down."

Mack slapped a hand on Ashton's shoulder. "You could get a job as one of those meteorologists. You just managed to say you have no idea using a whole bunch of pretty words."

The other man grinned. "This is when Kelli out at the ranch would say 'if you can't dazzle them with your brilliance, baffle them with your bullshit.'"

It only took a moment to get directions to the silo and barn where Ashton had heard the star was stored. "I mentioned you might be stopping by at some point, and Yoder said he was fine with it. Don't burn anything down."

"Yeah, because that's always an occupational hazard with me," Mack deadpanned.

Ashton's grin went extra-wide. "No, but it's commonly known that you and Brooke are a pair, which means she'll probably be by your side. That woman has a reputation for lighting bonfires in kitchens across the county."

That was one comment Mack had no intention of sharing with Brooke.

But the rest of it? He totally needed to have her by his side. He hurried to finish the final task of setting up the timer for the Christmas lights, and when he checked his watch it was just shy of four o'clock.

He wasn't going to message her—if she was in the middle of a task, she wouldn't answer anyway. If they wanted to do this, they needed to do it quick before they lost the light.

Mack was out at the shop in under ten minutes, marching in the door and glancing around to track down his favourite woman in the whole wide world. "Brooke?"

She popped up like a jack-in-the-box from behind a big Chevy dually. Her expression lightened, lips curling upward. "Hey. What're you doing?"

"Something," he teased. He marched across the shop floor, leaning down to whisper. "Where's your dad?"

"Went to the bank," she whispered back. "Does that mean I get a kiss right here in the shop?"

He picked her up and enveloped her in a hug, kissing her enthusiastically. Brooke wrapped her legs around his hips and clung tight, palms pressed firmly to his cheeks as she gave as good as she got.

It was so fucking perfect—only this wasn't the moment to get distracted.

He pulled away. "On a scale of one to ten, how much trouble are you going to be in if I steal you away right now?"

Curiosity and mischief lifted her expression. "Some kinds of trouble are completely worth it."

Bingo. "Come on a treasure hunt with me? I think I know where your dad's star is."

~

SHE LEAPT at the chance to take the adventure.

The decision was easier because she had finished her work list and wasn't leaving Dad in the lurch. She had enough presence of mind to jot a quick note and pin it where he was sure to see it before ditching her coveralls and joining Mack in the warm truck.

She slid next to him and curled her arm possessively around his biceps. "So, this treasure hunt. Tell me more."

"Ashton discovered that after the last time the star went up, they were doing renovations on the church storage facilities. All the bits and pieces got sent home with different families, and it was only afterward that they were brought back to be stored in the shed. A couple years later they returned them all to your dad and he put them in the attic."

"Except the star didn't make it back."

Mack turned onto a secondary road, putting the truck in four-wheel-drive to deal with the heavy snow that had not been cleared by the snowplows. "Somebody out at the Yoder ranch was sick or something, so they didn't return the star. Someone thought they'd seen it a couple years ago, though, so if it's still there, we might be in luck."

Outside, the sky was still bright, a beautiful winter day with sunlight dancing off the snow crystals. "It's a lot of work to go get back something that's not even going to be put up at our house."

Mack linked his fingers with hers. "But your dad

remembered it, and it meant something to him. Plus, I know for sure the people over at the seniors lodge are going to appreciate seeing it shining above their roof."

Then he told her a story about snowballs and Santa and sneaky ball throwers, and she was giggling by the time they pulled to a stop in front of a long approach to a distant barn.

The fence ran in a fairly straight line, the tops of the wooden posts sticking up like hopeful sprouts in the spring. Only, the road had obviously not been driven at all this winter.

"I guess that's the end of that," she said sadly. "We can come out in the spring and check if it's there. It'll be set up for next year."

"Oh, ye of little faith." Mack had his door open, glancing down at the road beside him. "It's just a little dusting of powder."

Brooke shuffled onto her knees to stare as he waded into the drifts. "Just a little? I feel the urge to make a joke about your inability to judge size, but that might end poorly."

Mack grinned. He offered his hand then guided her to where he had marched in a small circle and packed down the snow. "Come on. I told you it was going to be an adventure."

The sight of her bag in the back seat triggered an idea. "Fine, but I need to bring supplies."

He looked confused for a moment until she pointed. A nod of agreement followed. "That's a great idea."

He grabbed her bag and tossed it over his shoulder, then reached for his backpack, adjusting position so he could carry them both easily.

The truck was far enough off the road to make it safe if anyone else needed to pass while accidentally wandering down a remote impassable stretch of highway. Not likely, but still it was good to be safe.

Brooke grinned as she fell into step behind Mack, his big boots leaving a trail for her to follow.

"You're lucky I'm tall," she told him. "Taking shorter steps would make you look like a penguin shuffling through the drifts."

The sound of masculine laughter carried back to her and he glanced over his shoulder. "I like penguins."

"I know."

The conversation slid to their favourite animals and what they would do when faced with snow conditions like this, and the fifteen-minute trek to the barn passed quickly.

The man door was blocked by a snow drift that reached nearly to the top of the doorframe.

Mack glanced around then motioned for her to follow him a little further. "I have an idea."

His idea turned out to be a side window that swung inward when he pushed. It was easy to climb up because the drift was not only as high as the window ledge, it was hard-packed by the wind. Solid enough that Brooke scrambled to the top then shifted her feet over the sill to slide into the stillness of the barn.

Mack tossed the bags over one at a time before joining her.

Inside was only slightly warmer than out, the wind blocked by the sturdy wooden structure. Brooke listened, but the silence was the main sound besides the steady rhythm of Mack breathing.

The ceiling rose upward for two and a half stories, opening above their heads like a cathedral. The stillness wrapped around her, yet it wasn't frightening but awe-inspiring. Especially when Matt tugged off her glove so he could link their fingers together.

They stood there, the quiet a tangible thing.

When she finally spoke, it was in a whisper. "Wow. This is better than any church I've ever been to."

"It's damn fine," he agreed. "Want to go stargazing with me?"

"Nope." Although they would, soon. This was not the moment to be tromping around looking for even a vital part of the old-fashioned Christmas. This was a moment to savour.

Mack tilted his head in a question.

She pulled him against her and offered her lips.

He took the hint, cradling the back of her head and kissing her deep. Slow yet powerful as they connected after the time apart. Turning to each other in this place that felt beautiful and eerie at the same time.

Mack picked her up, his lips still caressing hers as he walked a couple of paces in the semidarkness. Barely enough light filtered in the various windows to let her see they were in a workshop space. Which meant it had to be a table of some kind that he rested her hips on before crowding against her and tugging their bodies even closer.

She dragged her fingers through his hair, careful of the scrape on his forehead. His toque fell to the ground unminded. They were more concerned with teasing each other—pressing kisses to her cheeks and his jawline.

He nipped at her lower lip then kissed it soothingly. "You have an amazing ability to make me lose my focus."

"Same. Let me remind you what we were doing—it involved kissing. We can get back to it anytime."

Foreheads touching, he stared into her eyes.

Then the quiet...rattled. The rattle...*whooshed.*

The small amount of light in the area around them went from faint to nothing between one breath and the next. Like a curtain had fallen, they suddenly stood in utter darkness.

A shriek rang out, wild howling like the neighbour's cats when they'd decided to hold a jamboree in the middle of the night. The temperature dropped noticeably.

Brooke turned toward the window at the same time as Mack. The latch he'd loosely closed sprang open, and the wind that rushed in was no gentle breeze but a pounding, demanding beast that whirled paper in the air and set the windowpane crashing.

The storm had returned.

12

He'd known better. Part of him had sensed they were pushing it coming on this wild goose chase in the first place, but the instant he had stepped into the barn, he'd felt the impending disaster.

Call it intuition or a soldier's premonition. Call it sensing the change in the barometer, but he knew something big was about to happen.

Something more than the wild urge he'd had a moment ago to blurt out his feelings before dropping to one knee. Because as perfect as it would've been, memorable moment and all, they had more important things to figure out first. Like how bad was the situation and what would it take to make it through the night?

"Let's do some surveillance," he offered casually, striding over to the window to poke his head out and get a better sense of what they were facing.

Something out of a horror flick, it appeared. The sky roiled as if evil magicians were tossing spells at each other. A high-speed, fast-forward rush of billowing black clouds and snow that lashed his face relentlessly.

Brooke was at his back, her hand resting at his waist as he backed up and latched the window firmly. "I take it it's not good."

He faced her square on, adjusting position so he could see her expression. "The storm must've been waiting just over the ridge. I don't know how it arrived so quickly, but let's not deploy to the truck. Not yet."

Amazingly, there was no real worry on her face. Just deep trust as she tipped her chin in acknowledgement. Then she smirked, leaning forward and speaking loud enough to be heard over the continued whistling of the wind. "You're sexy when you start the soldier-in-charge thing. Just saying."

Amusement bubbled up and he laughed. "Good that you like him, because I have a feeling he's going to show up a lot in the next thirty minutes."

"Reconnaissance?" When he nodded, she snapped upright and offered a salute. "Lead the way, cap. I guess if we're stuck here for a couple of hours, we may as well figure out the best place to bunker down. And who knows? We might find the star at the same time."

He headed to his backpack and pulled out the flashlight he'd tucked in the top. When he turned toward her, it was to note with amusement she'd just stepped back from her bag and now held a battery-operated lantern.

"Impressive," he said.

"I was never in the Boy Scouts, but it's good to be prepared." She wrinkled her nose. "I got stuck in a hotel room once when the power went off and it was no fun to be without lights. It's part of my emergency backup stash."

"I've never seen it before."

Brooke raised a brow. "We've never had the power go out on us before. Trust me, it's always been in my bag."

She took the hand he offered, and they walked side by side,

mitts and toques on, coats bundled up against the cold as they explored the main level.

"Wow. Now *that's* sexy." Brooke broke away from him to run a glove over the fender of an ancient tractor, the lineage of which he could only guess at since it had elliptical treads instead of tires. "Hello, sweet baby. What are you doing out here, all by yourself and alone?"

Mack surrounded Brooke from behind, wrapping his arms tight around her waist as he nuzzled the side of her neck. "Guess this means the truth is out. My competition has tank wheels and a bucket."

She snickered, leaning back far enough so she could press a kiss to his cheek. "Don't worry, there's room for both of you in my life."

That fluttering sensation in his gut and heart was back and it had nothing to do with the fact they were likely not only trapped for a couple of hours, but a lot longer.

"Do you think she works?" Mack asked the expert.

Brooke slid a little farther around the tractor, peering into the engine area without moving any of the metal plates. "Can't say, but at some point, I'm going to play with this beauty and see if I can't get her humming."

He caught her by the fingers and tugged her toward the stairway. "You keep talking like that and we're going to need to find a firm surface sooner rather than later."

She glanced at him in surprise, as if thinking back over what she said and still couldn't see what he was talking about.

"Never mind," he mumbled. "I'm the one with the dirty mind."

"But I like your dirty mind." She stopped as he blocked her path to the stairwell. "Don't tell me, you're going first to make sure it's safe."

He shook his head. "I'm pretty sure it's safe, but first one up is going to dislodge all the spiderwebs. You can be my guest if you'd like."

She gestured him ahead. "My knight in shining armour. Have at 'er."

The second story had a small office area and a larger hayloft that covered two-thirds of the area. But other than some office materials, there wasn't a lot in the place that didn't fit in an abandoned barn.

There also wasn't a lot to help them spend a comfortable night. The hay was old and musty, pockets of it animal-chewed or moldy from where condensation had dripped from the ceiling.

Mack was regretting his "wild adventure" idea.

Brooke turned toward him then sneezed. She braced herself as another three explosions followed before she pinched her nose and peered at him through watery eyes. "Downstairs, stat."

He guided her back to the main floor, frantically looking for a way to fix this.

Brooke headed back to her duffel bag, hauling out a hanky and clearing her sinuses from the dust or whatever had set her off. She blinked hard, offering him a faint smile. "Now you get to see me in all my glory—dust allergies for the win."

It wasn't anything she needed to worry about. "You're beautiful."

He said it sincerely, quietly. Or at least as quiet as he could with the entire building around them rumbling as if they were at the center of some end-of-the-world apocalyptic movie.

Her smile warmed him through. "You're good. I think I'll keep you."

Always.

It was the first thought that leapt to mind. It was exactly what he was going to tell her as soon as he could reassure her they weren't going to freeze to death.

Priorities sucked.

A soft sound escaped Brooke, and he followed her gaze to the back of the barn where, lo and behold, their missing star was propped up along the wall, the faintest glint of gold reflecting the lantern in her hand.

"Well done," Mack said as he caught her by the hand again and led her toward their target. It wasn't going to keep them warm tonight, but it was something to celebrate. He shone the lantern on it, admiring the smooth welding job Gary had done. "I can see why he's proud of it."

He reached to take it off the wall, but it didn't budge.

Brooke pointed downward. "The stand is bolted to the floor."

Mack squatted to examine the setup, and the flashlight revealed a most unexpected surprise. "You know anything about the Yoder family who own this barn?"

"Other than the fact that they've been in the community for ages? I don't know too much about them—they pretty much keep to themselves a lot of the time. They must have homeschooled their kids because I don't remember going to class with any of them."

"Would you consider them dangerous?" Mack slid some leaves and fallen hay away from the clasp he'd discovered.

"The *Yoders*? Dangerous, no. Just not very bubbly or jump-in-and-join-the-party types. I know they always contribute to community things like park development and after-school programs, even though their kids didn't go. And I remember Rose mentioning their name as one of the families who donate every year to the food bank."

Which meant this probably wasn't as dangerous as it could be, but still.

He checked out Brooke who was holding her lantern to try to see around him. "Do me a favour and back up about ten paces."

She hesitated before raising the lantern to light up her face so that her glare was visible. "What're you doing?"

"Humour me. I want to make sure everything is kosher."

She hesitated, but then stepped back, folding her arms over the lantern and watching him intently. "I expect a full report ASAP, cap. I don't like being kept in the dark."

He flipped open the trap door and her eyes widened. "If I'm right about what I found, you won't be in the dark for much longer."

He shone his flashlight down the hidden set of stairs that had appeared, moving quickly but staying alert for any sign of booby traps.

It only took a moment to discover his first inclination had been right, and it was with a lighter heart that he raced back up the stairs, calling to Brooke as he went. "It's okay. It's safe, and you're not gonna believe this."

She met him at the top, arms still wrapped around herself and her concerned expression exchanged for sheer curiosity. "What's at the bottom of the stairs?"

He let his happiness show. "It appears that the Yoders are firm believers in being prepared. As in, to the extreme."

Brooke's jaw dropped. "They're *preppers*?"

Mack stepped aside and gestured her forward. "Come and check out your quarters for the evening, ma'am."

THIS WAS COMPLETELY UNEXPECTED.

From lighthearted happiness during the trip in the sunshine, to the storm's arrival—the contrast had been a shock, but still normal everyday events that were easy for Brooke to comprehend.

Walking down a steep, narrow metallic stairway away from the howling wind was something out of a sci-fi novel.

Mack turned on the lights, and the impression of being in an otherworldly place continued. "An oval passageway?" she asked.

"Culverts, probably covered with concrete on the outside, which is why the acoustics in here are fantastic."

They hit an open metal door, the shape of it suspicious. Brooke glanced back at Mack for confirmation, shock in her voice. "Is this a *submarine* door?"

He grinned. "You can open it from this side if it's not locked, but it's got an airtight seal and is very secure from the other."

She stepped through the door, and the space around them grew wider. A larger culvert than the one that had been used for the passageway had been converted into the shelter itself.

"Bathroom first?" She glanced to the side and gasped. "Are you kidding me? They've got a full-size tub and shower down here."

Mack stepped forward and guided her around the corner to where six bunks, two on one side, four on the other, were neatly arranged. "I'd guess the structure has at least a ten-foot diameter, which means there's plenty of room for an entire family. And yes, bathroom first because having it at one end provides the most privacy if you're actually stuck in the shelter for any length of time."

The bunk space was followed by the main living quarters. Bench seating like at any Denny's restaurant on the left, and a desk on the right. A little farther down was an entertainment unit opposite a leather couch.

"I'm thinking as preppers go, this is pretty luxurious." Brooke stared in fascination.

He stepped ahead of her, the extra room on the kitchen floor giving him space to guide her toward another closed door. "You're going to be pretty thankful for that luxury in a few seconds."

He opened the door and pulled her through.

"There's a queen-size bed in here. Because of course there is." Brooke turned to him with a happy sigh. "Okay, you can plan my disasters any time."

He pulled her closer, pressing his lips to her temple and kissing her briefly. "Aw, you say the sweetest things. And I didn't even show you the best part."

"Better than a queen-size bed in a shelter that I'm going to assume you can heat more than the dust-filled barn above us?"

Mack made a face. "Maybe not better than that, but still pretty cool." He tugged her toward the end of the bed and indicated another round portal. "This is the hatch to the escape tunnel."

"Get out."

"I didn't have time to check for sure," he admitted. "But we need to deal with a few other things before exploring. You mentioned heat—give me a couple of minutes and I can figure that out."

"What about the air? Is it safe or are we just going to leave the door open? And do we have water?"

"I saw a master control panel. I'll have all the answers soon enough."

He went to work on one side of the living space while Brooke distracted herself by poking through the cabinets in the kitchen area. There was plenty of bottled water and dehydrated food. They weren't going to starve.

Mack interrupted her scrounging. "All systems are online. CO_2 sensors are working, and we have a full cistern of water. We're pretty much in the lap of luxury, and I feel comfortable using anything we need. I'll get in touch with the Yoders and replace anything we consume."

"You think they're going to be pissed we know this is here?" Brooke could imagine people who went to this extent might not be pleased to have their secrets uncovered.

"I'll deal with them," Mack assured her. "Like you said, they seem to be preparing, but not dangerous. I'll make sure Brad comes along as backup, and maybe Ashton, but I also have contacts from my days in the Air Force. I might be able to provide information on how to make this place even better. Trust me."

It was exactly what she needed to hear. With this so far out of her experience range, she let it go. "Now what?"

"We go back upstairs, take another look at what's happening outside, and then we make a final decision."

Heading up the steep stairs was like walking into a sound machine. Her ears had returned to normal after the time in the bunker, and now the whistling alone sliced in and over her, making goose bumps rise.

Brooke joined Mack at the window, but darkness had completely fallen, and the only thing visible against the shine of his flashlight was a sideways sheet of tumbling white.

She checked her phone. "No reception."

"I don't know if that's because of the storm or because we're out of range," Mack said.

"As the crow flies, we're not that far from town. I know we drove in a big circle to get here, but chances are the system is down. There's no way to get a message out."

"Will your dad be worried?" Mack asked.

She shook her head. "He'll assume I was over at the fire hall and decided to stay with you when the storm hit."

Big hands clasped hers for a moment. Mack examined her intently. "I think it's the safest if we stay in the barn and don't try to get back to the truck or drive anywhere, but it's up to you if we use the bunker or not."

"Gee, let me think for a minute. Dust-covered hay bales or what looked like a thousand-thread-count quilt on the bed." She tapped her lips. "I know, I'm just a glutton for punishment, but let's go pretend we're gophers."

He lofted their bags in the air and led them back to the hidden stairwell.

"At some point I'd like Dad's star back, but maybe I'll let you use that as a bargaining chip." Brooke slid past Mack and took the lead, the pressure in her eardrums easing instantly. "This is so weird."

The main compartment was noticeably warmer already. Brooke took a deep sniff. "Smells fresh."

Mack closed the door behind them, twisting the levers and sealing them in. He glanced up. "Just to make sure nobody sneaks up on us unawares. Let me go check the sensors, but the air does smell good."

A moment later he'd confirmed it. They were officially snug as a bug in a rug.

It wasn't the hotel they'd been booked into for two nights ago, but it was a chance to be alone. Absolutely alone, and Brooke suddenly felt nervous. The sensation was outrageous and wrong, but she lifted her gaze to his and it seemed he'd had the same realization. The alone bit.

His eyes were dark and his expression had gone serious. "Brooke."

She swallowed hard. No one was going to interrupt them. It was the perfect opportunity for her to tell him how she felt, but her tongue was stuck to the roof of her mouth and the words wouldn't come.

Stating their emotions wasn't a thing in her family. Not when her grandparents had been alive and not in the years since. She knew her Dad loved her. She loved him, but saying it...

Mack stepped closer, his fingers caressing her jawline as he stared into her face. "So serious. This is going to be fun, babe. And I know exactly what we need to do next."

"The soldier taking control again?" It was easier to tease than to slap at herself in annoyance for not being bold enough.

"Definitely taking control, and the first rule of hunkering down for the night is to get comfortable. Sheer fluke that we brought our bags, but I assume you've got something in there other than jeans."

Brooke brightened. "I do. But what do you mean sheer fluke? I brought my bag for a very important reason."

Mack raised a brow. "You knew we were going to be trapped for the night?"

She grabbed her bag from where she'd dropped it on a bunk and headed toward the master bedroom. "Maybe. Or maybe I'm a super-honorary Boy Scout and believe in planning ahead. I'll be right back with your surprise."

He laughed but headed for his bag as well.

She only took a second to glance around the bedroom—which was over-the-top-wild to find thirty feet under the ground. Instead, she dug into her duffel bag, thankful for the opportunity to change from her work clothes into the pretty things she'd packed for their getaway then never got to use.

Her cheeks flushed, but she went ahead and pulled on the bra and panty set, covering them with her soft sweatpants and T-shirt. Finally, she grabbed the magic ingredient she'd had hidden away as a surprise.

Returning to the living space just as Mack was tucking in his shirt, she stopped to admire the view. The cut of his light grey T-shirt and flannel pyjama bottoms made him look as if he were an elegant survivalist.

His smile as he took in her clothing was hot enough to set her pulse pounding deep inside her. "Hot damn. Brooke Silver dressed in soft cotton and I get to unwrap her at some point—it doesn't get any better."

Her heart kicked up a pace, but her lips curled involuntarily into a smile. "That's not your present, this is."

She thrust out a bag of miniature marshmallows.

13

Brooke was perfect. From the top of her ponytailed-head down to the fuzzy slippers she'd pulled on. Everything about her made him relaxed yet eager. The flawless mix of familiar and comforting created a craving that wouldn't go away.

She stood there, holding forward a bag of *marshmallows*, her smile brightening the room. She didn't care where they were—he knew that to his core. If they'd had to remain upstairs with the hay bales and dust, she would still have been looking at him that way, albeit accompanied by a few more sneezes.

It wasn't about where they were. It wasn't about having the picture-perfect setting like a spectacular sunset with impeccable surroundings. It was about them being together.

The truth was so big he could barely breathe.

He stepped closer, reaching into his pocket for the reason why *he'd* insisted on bringing his bag. "That's a pretty amazing present. How about we do a trade?"

Mack dropped to one knee in front of her, watching close enough to catch the moment her eyes widened. He lifted the box in the palm of his hand to her and waited.

She jerked her arms back, clutching the pillowy bag of marshmallows to her chest. "*What*? Mack?"

He swallowed around the lump in his throat, opening the lid on the box to let her see the ring inside. "There's a wild story behind this, and I'll tell you in a bit, but the most important part? I love you. I need you in my life, not just when we can find the time, but always and forever. Will you marry me?"

She was still squishing the marshmallows as if that would help keep her upright. "Ohmygawd. But I never... But I thought... Ohmygawdmygawdmygawd."

His bold and brave woman had been rendered insensible.

"Brooke?" Mack wiggled the ring box. "The soldier suggests you stick to the priorities. First you say yes, then we can play twenty questions."

Her gaze slowly rose off the ring and back up to his eyes, her smile widening. "Well, if you're going to be like that..." She tossed the bag of marshmallows onto the couch and threw herself into his arms. "Yes. Oh, hell, *yes*."

His fingers closed instinctively over the box, tucking it back in his pocket. He used his other arm to cradle her as their lips met in joyous celebration. The connection perfect as always, the hunger and happiness in her kiss matching his own.

Mack gentled the motion, striving to slow them down from their automatic high-speed romance. It was barely five o'clock and they would be there at least until morning. He could take as much time as he wanted.

As much time as he needed to prove to her that what he said—it wasn't just words. That *everything* in him worshipped her.

He deepened the kiss, lifting her in his arms to carry her into the back room. Laying her down and sliding over her without breaking the connection between their mouths.

The room was still cool, but a gentle flow of heated air brushed over their skin. With his elbows braced on either side of her head, hips nestled between her thighs, the two of them were warm enough to concentrate on touching. Caressing.

Being together.

Mack kissed his way from the corner of her mouth then up her cheek and over the upper edge of her ear. Brooke quivered under him.

He liked that but needed to interrupt before they got too involved. "One minute. We missed something."

His heart pounded as he sat back and pulled the ring from the box, slipping it onto the hand she offered him. They both stared for a moment, the pale pink gems flashing in the lights over the headboard.

"It's wonderful," she said.

Maybe. The amazing part was they had each other, and he was now free to spend every bit of his energy on her. Slow, slow, oh-so-slow.

"I'm going to worship you," Mack warned, licking her earlobe before drawing it into his mouth and sucking softly. "You're mine."

"You're mine, as well," she whispered.

"Yes, but I called first dibs."

As a puff of amusement escaped her lips, he dragged his teeth along the side of her neck. Her laughter turned into a moan, and then he was sliding a hand under her T-shirt to press his palm to her warm belly.

"All of you. I'm going to touch and taste and tease until you know exactly how much you mean to me."

"*Mack.*" It was a sound of desperation.

He pushed up the fabric of her T-shirt to reveal a pale blue bra, fine enough he could see her nipple through the fabric. If anything, he grew harder in anticipation.

Pulling her just high enough to strip away her top, Mack smiled in approval. "And look. Another present for me."

Her eyes were soft and hooded, slightly dazed from his

kisses. "You should keep looking. There might be a second part to the present."

That was encouragement if he'd ever heard it. Mack stripped away her sweatpants and stared down with his heart pounding at the sight of her long limbs and sweetly curved body wrapped in the smallest scraps of winter blue. "I must've been a very good boy this year."

"The best. And I should've told you that so many times."

The hint of sadness in her voice was completely wrong. Mack glanced up, shocked to see moisture in her eyes. "Hey—"

"I love you." The words spilled from her lips like a confession. "I have for a long time but never told you—"

He lay down and pulled her against him, squeezing her close as she inexplicably burst into tears. Quiet sobs that made her body rock and her breathing turn ragged. He caressed a hand down her back, pressing kisses to her face and lips while he muttered soothing words the best he could.

Mack held the most important person in his world until she found her equilibrium.

When she took a deep breath and let it out slowly, nuzzling under his chin like a feral kitten that had finally accepted a home, his heart felt as if it'd swollen to three times its normal size.

"I'm sorry. I don't know where that came from." Brooke tilted her head and met his gaze. "Maybe I do. I regret not saying something sooner. I should've told you how I felt a long time ago, but...I'm not used to saying it. We just don't."

He squeezed the hand now resting on her hip, sliding in a slow caress over her skin and warming her with his touch. "There's nothing to regret. For whatever reason, it took us until now, and we won't look back. Besides, we both need practice, because I could've said it a long time ago as well. I guess sometimes we just think people know how we feel about them."

Her lips touched his, a prayer and supplication at the same time. "I can handle practice. I love you, Mack. So, so much."

He used his thumb to wipe away a tear that clung to the corner of her eye. "I love you. And I'm going to *love* you. Thoroughly."

He rolled her under him and this time there was no sadness as he kissed his way to her lips and took greedily. Tangling their tongues and demanding a response as he braced himself over her, her lush body cradling him with acceptance.

Brooke pushed at his shirt, pressing her bare hands to his naked torso. He broke the kiss for long enough to reach up and jerk the fabric over his head before returning to the addiction that was kissing her.

He was still going to go slow even if it killed him.

She replaced her hands, curling her fingers over his shoulders and dragging her nails down his back and the sides of his torso. Warming all of the parts in him that said she liked what she touched and wanted more.

Wanted *him*.

She moaned in protest as he pulled away to rest his hip on the mattress beside her. He kissed her quickly in apology, but he was on a mission, staring down at her perfect breasts covered with the finest of lace. "So pretty."

He caressed first, just because he could. Small circles where the heat of her reached his fingertips and teased his senses with silky smoothness and sensual warmth. When she arched upward, pressing her breast into his palm, he pulled the cup back, plumping up the soft mound with the fabric underneath. Her nipple tightened and he brushed his thumb over the surface.

Brooke inhaled sharply.

He couldn't look away. She reacted perfectly to his touch, her body arching to meet him, moving with his strokes as if she couldn't bear to be separated from him. And when he leaned in close enough to press a kiss to the little white bow between the bra cups, Brooke clutched the fingers she'd tangled in his hair and tugged.

Laughter rumbled from inside him because where she was guiding him was exactly where he needed to go. Slowly, though. Oh, so slowly, licking and nipping as he made his way up the smooth underside of her breast to the peak.

He kissed the tip, and she squirmed.

Mack opened his mouth and pressed his tongue to the taut surface then closed his lips and sucked softly.

"*Yes.*"

Absolute approval, and Mack smiled. He took his time, switching from side to side, staying in control as he teased and licked. When he pulled back and blew gently over the wet surface, Brooke squeezed her fingers together and pulled his hair in retaliation.

He caught her wrists and placed her palms against the mattress. "Sensitive?"

"Greedy. I want more. I want you."

She attempted to reach for him, but he kept her locked in position. "It's not your turn yet. Keep your hands there."

The final words came out like an order, and her eyes widened briefly before her lips twitched. "Captain in the house."

"Captain on the bed. Don't worry, I'll let you know when it's your turn to do anything other than feel."

He leaned down and pressed a kiss to the center of her body, breathing in her sweet scent and preparing to get drunk on her pleasure.

THEY'D TURNED a corner in their relationship she'd hoped for someday but had never expected to arrive so soon or so completely. Even the way he touched her felt different. More deliberate, more meaningful.

Definitely intended to drive her wild.

Brooke tensed her fingers against the surface of the quilt as Mack teased his way down her body, kissing and caressing, sliding her thighs farther apart until he rested firmly between her legs. He stared down at the scrap of material masquerading as panties she was suddenly glad she'd purchased.

"These are sinfully soft." He brushed his lips over the fabric directly above her mound. A rush of pleasure radiated outward over her skin like a tingle of electricity. "I can get used to you wearing these all the time."

"Under my coveralls?"

His cheek slid toward her hip, his lips gliding along the narrow rim of elastic on the return journey. "Definitely. No one will know but us, but every time I stop off at the shop, I'll picture you like this. The way you give yourself to me wholeheartedly while no one else gets to see this side of you. So pretty and feminine and smart and capable."

Brooke lifted her heel and ran her bare toes along his muscular shoulders. "Sweet talker."

"It's true." His gaze met hers straight on, passion rising in his gaze. "You're distracting me."

"I hear multitasking is a thing."

She wasn't quite sure why that made him grin as hard as he did, but then she wasn't thinking very hard because he tucked a finger in the edge of her panties and peeled them away.

What followed was an exercise in how to lose focus in the best way possible. Mack pushed her knees higher, pressing a kiss to her inner thigh before nipping lightly. The other side got the same treatment then his tongue slowly slid upward until he was just shy of where she needed him.

He brushed his nose through her curls, hands moving under her hips to lift her to his mouth.

One lick, slow and teasing. Not enough pressure, not enough anything to do more than make her want to squirm. But she couldn't because he had an ironclad grip on her hips.

He glanced up, a smile on his wicked mouth as he did it again. A little deeper through her folds, pausing at the apex long enough to let her know exactly where he planned to spend some time.

Brooke clutched the quilt and prepared for a long ride.

If he'd intended to continue the torturously slow pace, though, he wasn't succeeding. It was as if every time he touched her he lost a little control. He pulled her hips closer to the edge of the bed, pushed her knees toward her head, and got down to business as if his entire goal was to see how quickly he could send her over the edge.

Pretty damn fast.

The spiraling heat from his tongue flicking against her clit sent those lightning bolts flying through her belly again, tension building at such a rapid pace that when he slid a finger into her sex, she came.

He rumbled in approval as she rocked against his mouth, licking softer but continuing to work her until the climax came off the crescendo.

When she would've reached for his shoulders to pull him over her, he didn't move, just started up all over again. Two fingers entered her body, his fingertips teasing a spot inside that made her press a hand to her mouth to hold back a cry of pleasure.

He must've glanced up because he stilled for a second before his fingers carried on the rhythm and he spoke, a growl in his voice as if he were the one trying to keep from screaming in pleasure. "Don't you dare try to stay quiet. There's no one here to overhear us, and dammit, I want it all. I want your pleasure and your voice calling my name, letting me know exactly what I've done to you."

Brooke gasped as he put his mouth back over her and consumed her as if she were oxygen and he were a fire. "Mack, oh my *God*."

"Give it to me."

Pressure was flaring again, but she didn't want to go over without him. "Please, I need you. I want you inside me. I want your cock."

His rhythm skipped for a second, then he moved. Stripping down and covering himself as she slid back on the mattress to make room. He was over her, dragging her leg above his hip as his cock nudged at her center.

His thickness poised at her core, he lifted up and caught her gaze. "I love you."

Mack said it as if it was fact. As if the love between them was titanium strong and bombproof. His eyes said it as well as his words, and Brooke pressed her palm to his face and offered her pledge as well. "I love you too."

He slid home.

Familiar, yet different. Heated pleasure with the cool wave of electric sensation along her nerve endings that said another orgasm was building. He moved in her, eyes locked with hers, breathing accelerating. She wrapped her legs around his firm hips, her heels pressing into his buttocks.

She clutched his shoulders as he picked up the pace. Not enough to be wild and out-of-control, but long steady strokes that made both of them moan.

"So close," Brooke whispered.

Mack leaned on one elbow, bringing his hand to his mouth and licking his fingers. He reached between their bodies and found her clit. Teasing and stroking even as he kept his hips rocking in a perfect rhythm. A connection between their bodies that was more than just physical.

He was gazing into her eyes as the tsunami hit. Less of an explosion this time, yet more powerful and overwhelming. Her body tightened down around his, and a sound broke free from his lips. Something between a prayer and a shout. As his shoulders tightened, his hips stuttered to a stop, leaving him buried deep.

Brooke closed her eyes as another wave hit, this one with added emotional impact as she realized the whispering sound was Mack repeating "I love you" over and over again.

Her heart pounded and her breath was shaky, but as she looked up to see the most important part of her heart staring down at her, she knew she'd experienced something amazing. A beginning she would never forget.

He leaned in and kissed her again. Soft, sweet, although that imagery was probably way off base considering the connection between them remained heavy and hot between her legs.

"Wow. That was—"

"Yeah, it was." He kissed the tip of her nose then rolled them, putting her on top so she could sprawl as if boneless over his muscular frame.

They lay there for a while, breathing synchronized, hearts slowly returning to normal pace. Mack pulled the edge of the quilt over her, but the heat rising from his body left her warm as well as sated. Guarded in his arms, satisfaction simmering through every part of her.

It wasn't until his stomach growled that she reluctantly pushed upright. He still held her, but his grin was back. The one that said mischief might be in store.

"I guess it's time to check out the emergency supplies," she said. "But I suggest you might want to do the cooking. I have no problem lighting fires in my own stove, but I don't think it's a good idea to push our luck here."

They slipped out of bed and Brooke stole Mack's T-shirt to make a quick trip to the bathroom.

By the time she rejoined him in the kitchen, Mack had also

cleaned up and pulled on a spare shirt. There was a pot on the stove, flame underneath it, and a collection of packages laid on the counter.

Only it was the ziplock bag that caught her attention. "Are those cookies?"

"They're not from the stash of food here," he assured her. "I made them for our night away, which we're finally getting to enjoy."

She cracked open the bag, and the rich scent of spicy goodness filled the room. "Hmmm, snickerdoodles. Something about these makes me drool just thinking about them."

"It's entirely possible the old-fashioned cookies you're attempting to make are some distant relative to these."

Brooke eyed the one she held in her fingers, breathing appreciatively although a small trace of sadness snuck into what had turned out to be an amazing evening. "This is going to be the lamest old-fashioned Christmas ever. I never did get the baking figured out."

"No, but you did find the Christmas music, and we're going to have homemade gifts, and we'll still have a special meal and time together." He turned and brought her against his body, biceps strong as he cradled her close. "And maybe your dad will be excited that we're getting married."

She nodded slowly. "I know he's grumbly, but he does like you."

"It'll work out," Mack assured her before drawing her attention to the assortment of dehydrated food he'd found for them to pick from.

It was true. They'd already done the hard work for them— admitting they'd fallen in love. Whatever they did from here on, they'd do it together.

Once the storm let them return to the real world.

14

The shelter made it feel as if they'd stepped into another dimension. Mack found that both eerie and fascinating, but the most important part was they were safe and they were together. He found the music system and used Bluetooth to get his own playlist carrying through the cozy space.

No sounds carried from the storm, no vibrations, and the warmth coming from the radiant heat turned their surroundings T-shirt comfortable.

It was an idyllic place to celebrate the change in their world.

They talked about ordinary things while they ate the dehydrated meal, which was better than the rations Mack had eaten during his Air Force days. But afterward, Brooke tugged him to the couch with her, curling up next to him and wrapping her arms around his torso. Her hair spread over his chest, and he ran his fingers through it, sensual silk he wished was touching his skin.

"How do you want to do this?" she asked. "I mean, what's the next step after the storm stops and we get out of here? Plus the bit after that where we figure out how to be together."

"We can start looking for a place to rent." He pressed a kiss to the top of her head, still petting her slowly because he could. "Part of the reason why I didn't say anything sooner was the cheap accommodations at the fire hall. I've been helping my parents make their mortgage payments for the last year. They made a few unwise decisions, but they'd committed to getting out of debt, and I didn't want to see them have to declare bankruptcy."

She sat upright, concern on her face. "Are they okay? They're out in Ontario, right?"

"Oshawa. And yes, I think they got behind on some payments when Dad lost his job a couple years ago. Mom's military pension isn't huge, but with the two of them working again, they were doing okay. Late last year, they admitted they were in trouble and I figured, with the great deal I was getting at the hall for board, I could afford to help them out." He stroked his knuckles over her cheek, amazed that she'd agreed to be his. "I didn't expect to meet you, but once I'd made the commitment to them, I couldn't back out."

"Of course not," she agreed. "I thought you were paying off student loans—that's where all my extra money has been going. I made the last payment at the start of the month. I was planning to ask in January if you wanted to find a place with me that didn't involve living with my dad."

Mack shook his head. "Stupid finances. We could've been together so much earlier."

She shrugged. "You said we weren't going to look back, so we'll look the other direction. But I'm proud of you for helping your folks."

The warmth came because of her words and the way that she said them, not because of any pride about what he'd done. "They're good people and not too in-your-face. But they know about you, and they're looking forward to meeting you."

Brooke nodded slowly. "My dad will be okay in the

apartment by himself, but are you okay staying in Heart Falls? You're not going to get stationed somewhere else, are you? I know you're not going back on active duty, but even civilian firefighters sometimes get transferred."

A sudden rush of deep emotion hit as he realized she'd said yes to him without knowing for sure where they might end up in the future. "I would never take you away from your dad or your job. If you vanished, half the vehicles in Heart Falls would stop running."

She grinned. "Maybe a third."

Her hand lay over his heart, and he caught her wrist and lifted it so he could examine the ring. It was a little big, so she'd slipped it on her middle finger, but the pale pink stones glittered beautifully as she twisted her hand to admire it.

"Do you like it? I know some women like to pick their own rings, and we still can, but this one wanted to come home to you."

Her eyes widened. "You said there was a story. Tell me."

So he shared about the day that every time he turned around there'd been another jewelry store mocking him. Displays in windows that showed stunning brunettes staring with love into dark-haired men's eyes, and made him realize that needed to be him and Brooke, stat.

She lifted her hand and examined the ring a little closer. "But this isn't a new ring. I thought you were going to tell me it was from your parents or your grandparents."

"Well, it's from *somebody's* grandparents," he admitted. "I resisted the urge to purchase anything at those fancy stores. I figured once I asked you, I could take you to one and see what you liked. But fate had other ideas."

She was leaning forward now, eager for the rest of the story like a kid waiting for Santa to arrive.

"Yup, once the idea of getting you a ring had been raised, there was no way I was going home without one, fancy stores be damned. I had to make one final stop, safely away from any jewelry shops, and discovered a thrift store next door. I only grabbed some T-shirts, but as I was chatting with the fellow behind the cash register, he suddenly got all shifty-eyed and nervous, as if he was about to do something illegal. When he reached under the counter, I thought for sure he would pull out a stash of drugs. I couldn't figure out what I'd said to make him think I was interested in anything like that."

Brooke was laughing now, her body warm against his, their fingers tangled. "Did you look extra disreputable that day or something? Because hello, clean-cut soldier boy."

"I swear I was perfectly normal. I was also very relieved when he brought out a mostly empty TV tray with a couple of pieces of jewelry on it and said, 'We don't put this stuff on display, but I feel as if the universe is telling me to show them to you.'" Mack imitated the laid-back drawl the man had, grinning at Brooke's expression. "I guess sometimes jewelry shows up in the pockets of clothing that gets donated or in luggage. This time they knew who it belonged to because they'd just unpacked a load that had come from an estate sale. When they contacted the family to give back the more valuable items, they were told to keep them as a donation."

Her eyes were bright, and her lips twisted upward. "You bought my ring at a thrift store. Not that I'm knocking it, I think that's kind of cool, but just to make sure I've got the facts straight."

"I definitely bought your ring at a thrift store, although I did give them a good amount."

"More than ten bucks?"

He grinned. "At least twenty. You're worth it."

She snickered. "So, can you tell me anything else about my ring? Because I do like it, and it's pretty. But I don't think you would've just bought it because somebody suggested you should."

And this was part of the reason why he loved her. She understood there was a deeper meaning.

He lifted her fingers to his lips and kissed them slowly. "A ring is a sign of commitment, but this one is also a symbol of *us*. I wanted something unique and not like all the rest that will be purchased this year. This has been around for a while, and it's proven it can stand the test of time."

"You know that?"

Everything in him went soft with memory. "The couple had over sixty years together. I think that's a pretty good goal to start with."

She held her hand up and wiggled her fingers, considering. "But I'm not going to be haunted by some woman named Ethel who wants her ring back?"

"Definitely not," he answered instantly. "Her name was Dorothea."

Laughter burst free from Brooke and she adjusted position to kneel on either side of his thighs, hands resting on his shoulders. "Well, that's good." She leaned forward and brushed her lips over his. "I love my ring, and I love that story, and I love *you*. You chose well."

As the evening rolled into night, and they held each other and once again made love, Mack could not find a single thing wrong with her proclamation.

Being together with her there in the bunker was only the start.

He woke early the next morning, reluctantly slipping out of bed and away from Brooke's warmth to check their status. He was barely to the top of the stairs when the shrieking sound of the wind was enough to warn him the storm was still raging.

He checked both their phones for reception before giving up and returning to the safety of the bunker.

When he crawled back into bed, Brooke gasped slightly before pressing her warm body against all his chilled parts.

"We still trapped?" she asked sleepily.

"Very."

She twisted toward him, nuzzling against his chest. "Important question to ask."

"I thought I already did that."

She smirked, lashes at half-mast. "How many days can we survive?"

"Depends," he admitted. "How many condoms did you stick in *your* emergency pack? Because at the rate we're going, we'll need to hike for safety in the next twenty-four hours or be in trouble."

An amused *hmmm* escaped her lips as she placed a hand on his chest, manoeuvering his back to the mattress so she could slide over him. "Then we're good for at least another day and a half." She reached into their stash and held one in the air. "Are we rationing ourselves?"

Easy answer. "Hell no."

He waited until she'd tortured him by gloving him up, then rolled, guiding her onto her side so he could caress her breasts while keeping pressed tight against her back. A slow, languid loving followed. His cock snuck between her legs from behind and teased against her sex until she was rocking her hips back as if begging for more.

When he slipped inside her, moving with an easy rhythm, it was flawless. Pleasure building, urgency rising until they both came apart. He cradled her against him, intimate and joined, as she trailed her fingers over his hands, his forearms. Back over his hip to tease the naked skin of his buttock as if she couldn't stop and didn't want to break the connection between them.

He pressed a kiss to the back of her neck. "I love you."

It sounded as perfect as it had all the other times.

~

It was a little like having a honeymoon without having to deal with the wedding formalities. Although Brooke had never seen a destination resort quite like their prepper shelter.

They kept going upstairs every few hours to check the weather situation, but if anything, Mother Nature had chosen Christmas Eve to be worse than what had been thrown at them on the twenty-third.

Brooke had teased until Mack pulled on his full winter gear, and the two of them went outside, tucking around the corner to get out of the raw fury of the wind.

"The only reason we're doing this is because I'm heavy enough not to get blown away," Mack informed her, keeping a firm grip around her waist as they stood in the leeward side of the shed and stared across the field through the brief gaps in the whiteout.

"It's not what I want to deal with every day, but it's weirdly invigorating to be out here," she shared before they retreated into the cold but windless interior of the barn.

She poked at the tractor for a few minutes, admiring its classic John Deere lines, but she went willingly when Mack tugged her toward the star and the warmth hidden below it.

The entire day vanished in the most wonderful of ways. Mack insisted they take advantage of all the amenities, which meant hot showers and breaking out the games. Although he did suggest they conserve water and shower together.

Their stack of condoms rapidly diminished, and she'd never seen Mack so relaxed and happy.

They did talk about the people who would be missing them, but even there Brooke couldn't feel too concerned. "My dad knows you'll take care of me."

"Your dad knows you'll take care of *me*," Mack pointed out. He made a face. "I tried to generate some guilt about not being in Heart Falls for emergency services, but this is why we trained the extra volunteers. Plus, I just heard somebody very wise suggest no one should be irreplaceable."

She slid up to him then, hands cupping his cheeks as she stared into his beautiful eyes. "At work? I agree. But when it comes to being in my heart, I don't want anyone but you."

For some reason her words triggered another tumble into bed.

Oops?

But when they went to bed on Christmas Eve still trapped by the storm, she had to admit she was a little disappointed.

"I hate to sound like a broken record, but the weather is screwing up our plans. If the storm lets up, and *if* we can get your truck started, and *if* we can get back to town, any chance of that old-fashioned Christmas I was hoping for is gone by now." She wrapped her arms around her legs, pouting into the semidarkness. "Bah, humbug."

Mack pressed a kiss to her arm, trailing his fingers softly over her torso. "We can have turkey for New Year's. Because you're right, it's still frozen solid so there's no way we're eating that tomorrow even if we do get to make a break in the morning."

His fingers slid into a ticklish area and she attempted to wiggle away. "I forgot—I was going to suggest we go to the seniors lodge on Christmas Day. I think Geraldine and Floyd would enjoy the company."

"Great minds think alike," he told her. "I had the same thought when I was there setting up the Christmas decorations. And if by some chance we're still stuck at the end of tomorrow, we'll go the next day. Or the next. They'll appreciate the company whenever we make it."

"We could probably tell Floyd it was still Christmas a week later and he'd be okay with it. So, it's not as if it's the actual date that's the important part," Brooke said softly, understanding filtering in.

It really wasn't about a random date on a chart, but who she spent it with.

The tickling turned more earnest and they ended up giggling like a pair of kids before the playing turned a lot more adult.

Christmas morning arrived, and Brooke woke earlier than Mack. She slipped out of bed to explore, only to rush back and bounce on the edge of the bed. "Wake up, wake up."

"I wanted to open my present in bed," he complained, reaching for her but missing as she danced out of his grasping hands.

"Later," she told him excitedly. "Come listen."

He groaned but obediently followed to the exit door. She swung it open then pressed a finger over her lips.

"I don't hear anything." Mack's eyes widened. "Oh. I don't hear anything."

He hurried up the stairs, Brooke hard on his heels, and they headed for the nearest window.

It was early enough that the sky had just begun to brighten, the sunlight not yet reaching to the top of the mountains to the west. But the fact they could *see* the mountains was the little Christmas miracle she'd been hoping for.

Brooke twirled in his arms and pulled him close. "Merry Christmas to us."

His grin said it all before he kissed her passionately.

On the way back to the kitchen to grab a quick meal before they made their escape, Mack stopped beside the entertainment unit. "Where did those come from?"

She tried for innocent as he pointed to the brightly coloured socks hanging at eye level. "Well, I'll be damned, Santa made it."

He glanced at her and grinned. "You should've told me."

"Me? No. See, it was *Santa*. There's his empty glass and the cookie plate I left for him last night." She'd consumed most of the snickerdoodle after breaking off the teeniest crumb to leave it decorating the plate.

She took down one stocking and passed it to him. Mack peered inside before carefully lifting out the little stick figures and tiny buildings she'd made by pushing toothpicks through the miniature marshmallows.

"Awww, there's a fire truck. And a house, and some tiny people." He grinned at her. "You and me?"

She nodded.

Mack shook his head in amusement then reached for the other sock, his expression turning confused as he discovered it wasn't empty. "You goof. You loaded your own stocking."

"It wasn't me," Brooke insisted. "That Santa, he's a naughty old elf."

She upended her stocking and shook it, and a dozen of their condom stash fell into his hand like an adult snowfall.

He pulled her against him and kissed her enthusiastically, his lips still curled in a smile. When they both came up for air, he offered her a look that held all sorts of promise. "Let's put your present away. I promise we'll enjoy every bit of it later, but I think we should get out of here while we can, in case the storm returns for round three."

They split up the tasks. Brooke pulled things together and tidied the bunker while Mack made his way out to the truck to see if it would start.

"There's no use in both of us wading through the snow if I can't get it going. And while I spotted spare batteries and jumper cables, I'm not going to haul them out if I don't need them."

Brooke decided to take the bedsheets and linens that needed to be washed with them so she wasn't leaving more work for the Yoders. Plus, they'd made a list of everything they'd used, so by the time Mack made it back to the barn she had both their bags filled to the brim and waiting.

The disappointment on his face made it clear trouble wasn't done with them.

"Truck won't start?"

He shook his head. "Come with me. I'll bring the batteries if you bring the cables. You might know some other tricks to get her going. At least now there's a trail for us to walk."

She joined him outside, the sunshine brightening the sky and glittering off of the millions of crystalline snowflakes. The air was shockingly cold, bracing against the back of her throat.

Brooke couldn't help but smile even as they hooked up the battery and still couldn't get the truck engine to turn over.

"Why are you grinning?" Mack leaned across the open hood of the truck, his eyes flashing at hers with laughter in their depths.

She touched her nose to his. "Because I'm with you. Because I'm happy."

"You're stuck with me too," he pointed out.

"Bring the battery. I have another idea."

He followed her back to the barn. She'd had something percolating for the last while, and now with his cooperation, she cleared a path around the ancient John Deere plow.

Mack watched as she opened the engine compartment and squatted to get a good look. "You're kidding me. You think this thing still works?"

"We'll find out soon enough. She's old, but these things were built to last, and I don't mean that as a company catchphrase."

She found the master switch and flicked it on before hooking up the jumper cables. "We need to top her up with gas, and I need a pair of work gloves. This model has an open carburetor with a direct feed to the engine, so I need to cover the end to create enough vacuum to get the engine going."

They both scrounged around until they found a jerry can to transfer some purple farm fuel into the engine. Mack was the one who discovered a pair of worn leather gloves tucked into a drawer by the work bench.

She slipped them on and offered a wink. "Fingers crossed."

Brooke opened the fuel line then placed her protected hand over the end of the carburetor. She jimmied the starter cable, listening to the sound of the engine turning over, harsh at first before it fell into the smooth *putt-putt-putt* of an old two-stroke engine.

She stood, delighted at her success, and found herself picked up and whirled in a happy embrace.

"You're brilliant," Mack told her. "Which means it's time for us to get bundled up. This trip could take a while."

Not nearly as long as he thought. She helped gather their things and tucked them onto the tractor so they weren't in the way and wouldn't fall off.

They got the barn door open with a little work—thank God for sliding doors that moved with only a little clearance. Then she had the tractor outside and idling as Mack climbed up to join her.

He pointed toward the highway. "Adventure, ahoy."

She grabbed his wrist and changed the angle of his arm, his finger now pointing over the snow-covered fields that dipped and rose in waves toward the barely visible church tower at the edge of Heart Falls.

"That way, cap."

He swung around far enough to look intently into her eyes as if gauging if she was joking. "There's a heck of a lot of snow that way, babe, but if you think we can make it..."

"As the crow flies, we can definitely make it. And with this much snow, there's not a fence between here and the edge of town that's going to stop us. It'll still take a while, but we've got enough gas, and it's a beautiful day for a drive," she said with amusement.

His strong arms wrapped around her as he settled in the

back, letting her take control of the wheel and pedals. "Take us home," he ordered.

Mack squeezed her tight as she put the tractor into gear and the ancient treads began a steady elliptical motion, carrying them forward over the masses of fresh snow.

Carrying them home toward Christmas.

15

By the time they reached the edge of town, Mack's cheeks were sore from grinning. They'd begun to see people out and about on this festive day, and all of them stopped to stare as Brooke drove the old tractor in its highest gear—which was no more than a fast walk—down Heart Falls' Main Street toward the shop.

The slow pulse of the old-time engine beat out its steady rhythm like a little drummer boy, and Mack thought it was one of the most magical sounds in the entire world.

"I might have to see if the Yoders want to sell her." Brooke lowered the plow bucket and pushed a beautifully clear path across the width of the parking lot before putting the beast into park.

They didn't even have to go inside to know Gary wasn't home. Brooke pointed at the open spot where her dad usually parked his vehicle, a frown folding her expression at the tire tracks left in the snow. "You think he went looking for us?"

Mack had his phone out and was checking for messages. "I'm still not getting any reception, so whatever went down, went down hard."

Brooke pushed open the exterior door, checking her phone quickly before nodding in agreement. "I use a different server, and mine is down too." Both hands on the railings, she took the stairs two at a time. "Dad. You here?"

Mack followed her up in time to see her pick up a piece of paper left on the table.

She read it out loud. "*Figure you guys will get back sometime today. I'll be over at the seniors lodge helping out. If you don't get this, I'll track you down later. You better not have run away from home again.*"

The two of them glanced at each other then burst out laughing.

Brooke shook her head as she wiped tears from her eyes. "Good to know he wasn't sitting here worried sick."

"When did you run away from home?" Mack asked.

"I was five. It was naptime and Gram had taken away my toy toolset, so I decided I should go live at the shop where I could have all the hammers and wrenches I wanted." She motioned toward her room. "Let's grab a quick shower and a change of clothes to get rid of the diesel fuel smell before we head to the lodge."

There was no fooling around this time, just a quick scrub and a clean set of clothing Mack grabbed out of his duffel bag. They were in Brooke's truck and headed over to the seniors lodge double-quick, joining the other vehicles parked along the roadway.

The rooftop ornaments were barely visible under the new snow that had fallen in the last two days.

Inside, it smelled like Christmas.

Christmas carols carried over the sound system, and as it was just past lunch, something savoury lingered in the air. Brooke linked her fingers with Mack's, and they walked together down the corridor to where he'd met on the sly with Geraldine a few times this past month.

The common room was filled with small groups of people, some gathered around tables, some with chairs pulled close to wheelchairs and making their own little parties.

Gary Silver sat at a table with Geraldine and Floyd. Yvette stepped into view, a tray covered with teacups in her hands.

Her eyes lit up as she saw them. "You're back."

Gary's casual, relaxed state vanished as he shot to his feet and rushed over to envelop Brooke in an enormous hug. Without saying anything, he turned and caught Mack in an equally powerful embrace, slapping him on the shoulder before stepping back.

Gary turned his attention to Brooke. "You should've just told me you didn't feel like cooking for Christmas."

She rolled her eyes exaggeratedly before grinning. "It was far easier to get trapped in the snowstorm than have to face the wrath of the holiday fairies for destroying a Christmas turkey."

Her father draped his arm around her shoulders and turned them toward Geraldine and Floyd. "My kids are back safe, so I guess this means the party can start."

Mack paused for a minute, uncertain he'd heard the man correctly, but he followed the others to the table and settled at Brooke's side. Yvette brought two more cups, and they passed around a huge pot of tea and a plate filled with both mincemeat and butter tarts.

Floyd picked one up and eyed it, sniffing carefully before offering a shrug. "Looks good but not as good as *my* cookies."

Gary lowered his voice and leaned closer to Mack. "I figured you two were together, so you'd be okay. Anything I need to know?"

He wasn't about to tell Gary about the shelter until he'd had a chance to touch base with the Yoders. And he wasn't about to spill the beans about proposing because he figured Brooke would want to announce that.

But there was one thing Mack could share. "Your daughter

hot-wired a classic John Deere snowplow for our getaway vehicle. She's talking about buying it."

Gary's expression barely flickered, and his lack of reaction made Mack wonder exactly how much mischief Brooke could get into if she tried.

Then her father nodded. "Glad you kids are okay."

Across the table from them, Brooke had brought out the large iPad where she'd bookmarked the Christmas song. She propped it on the table in front of Geraldine and Floyd, gesturing her father closer. "It's not much, but I was trying to track down some old memories and found this. I hope you like it."

She hit play, and the soft sound of a woman singing began. Mack had watched the video enough times he recognized a few words, but mostly it was the amazing purity of the singer's voice that carried the beauty and the deep emotion of the holiday season. It was as near to perfection as he'd ever heard.

Until the next miracle happened.

Geraldine began singing along, her voice lower enough to be a complement to the original. Mack met Brooke's gaze across the table. She took a deep breath, happiness welling up in her expression.

Floyd blinked a couple of times. Then with no other preamble, he joined in.

If the soloist had been perfection, and Geraldine's voice something beyond that, Floyd's singing lifted the experience to nothing shy of heavenly. The old man closed his eyes, rocking slightly in his chair as he sang. His voice was crystal clear, with each word jewel-faceted and crisp. No hesitation, no faulty memories—he went through the entire song confident and sure.

Gary and others in the room had also joined in. Softer, more like background singers, as Brooke glanced in amazement at what her small gift had wrought.

Mack sat in silence and soaked in the joy.

To the side, Gary was still singing, furtively wiping away tears. He was trying to do it on the sly, the way many guys did, and as he turned from the crowd, his gaze fell on Brooke, who was unabashedly using a tissue to mop *her* face.

The bright lights sparkled briefly on the ring Mack had given her, now properly located on her fourth finger.

Gary stilled. Straightened.

He twisted immediately and caught Mack's gaze, his expression unreadable.

When the music faded, there were a lot of happy people in the room.

Once the hugs were finished, Gary motioned to Brooke and Mack. "I need to talk to you kids. Somewhere private."

Brooke came along willingly, but finding a quiet hallway was harder than Mack had imagined. Eventually they were tucked in a corner, the window to outside framing a small pine tree covered with teeny red balls.

"What's up?" Brooke whispered, but Mack shook his head and pulled her to his side, turning her to face her father.

The older man looked miserable and happy at the same time, if such a thing were possible. Gary dragged a hand through his hair.

He glanced at Brooke then back at Mack, then shook his head slowly. "You'd think by this stage of life I would have this being-a-dad thing figured out, but it looks as if I screwed up again. With good intentions, mind you, but still."

Brooke frowned. "What did you do?"

"Waited too long to tell you something." Gary met Brooke's gaze. "I'm proud of you. You've worked hard over the years, and I appreciate what you've done to make the shop a success *and* all the things you've done to make my life easier. You're not a bad roommate, either, but you deserved more. Especially once it became obvious that you were serious about this one."

He jerked a thumb toward Mack.

Mack held his tongue but still wondered why Gary refused to say his name.

Gary continued. "You kids are getting married, yes?"

The warmth of Brooke's smile lit up the entire alcove. She put her hand forward for her dad to examine. "We're very excited."

"Congratulations." He paused and changed the topic completely. "You know where you're going to live?"

"We figured we'd deal with that after the holidays," Mack told him. "But it'll be here in Heart Falls. We're staying close."

Gary seemed to be swallowing hard, and suddenly Mack wasn't finding this easy either.

It was clear exactly how much Gary Silver loved his daughter. When Gary took Brooke's free hand in his and squeezed tight, there wasn't much that Mack wouldn't do at that moment to make either of them happy.

"What if I told you I have a house for you?" Gary grinned a little at Brooke's gasp. "It's why I'm kicking myself, because I should've told you earlier. We've been renting out the house on Elm Street for years. When I saw you kids were getting serious, I made sure the renters knew they would have to be out when their lease expired. Unfortunately, that isn't until the end of December."

Brooke was speechless.

Mack was almost there as well, but he managed to squeeze out the question. "You have a *house* for us?"

"The house where we lived with Gram and Grandpa. It's not fancy, but it's got good bones, and it's big enough for you to stay for a number of years."

Brooke clenched Mack's arm. He glanced down at her. Saw the love in her eyes and the joy shining out from her very soul.

"What do you think?" he asked.

WHAT DID SHE *THINK*?

The roller coaster of a day wasn't giving Brooke much of a chance to breathe, and her head was so filled with unexpected happiness, she was grateful for Mack's arm around her giving her a wall to brace against.

She looked between them—the father who'd raised her and cared for her on his own for so many years, and the sturdy soldier who'd come into her life a year ago and filled it with everything that had been missing.

"I think it's outrageous and absolutely perfect. And I think, Dad, you need to know that you're the best, and there's absolutely *nothing* wrong with your timing." She glanced into Mack's deep brown eyes. "We weren't ready before, but we are now. We're ready to do the next thing."

She faced her father again, and he was grinning at the two of them as if he had something to do with getting them together.

"Thank you," Mack said, hand extended.

"You're welcome." Gary accepted the handshake and Brooke's hug, then he tilted his head toward the common room. "We better get back before Floyd sends out a search party."

Back in the common room, the atmosphere had jumped up a notch. All the residents there that day had gathered. Brightly coloured packages were being carried around the room, and as Brooke sat next to Geraldine, she was surprised to have a gaudily wrapped gift pressed into her hands.

Brooke stiffened in surprise. "Oh. I didn't know we were exchanging gifts."

Geraldine waved it off. "You brought the song for me and Floyd. That's more than enough of a gift." She wiggled her fingers excitedly. "Open it. Open it."

Brooke did as ordered, carefully slitting the tape and folding back the worn wrapping paper so it could be reused.

Inside the box was a familiar blue enamel cup. "I've seen this before," Brooke said uncertainly. "I think I remember…"

"Sharon said it was her favourite cup. It was the only one she ever used when she cooked."

Memories struck again. The pretty blue cup in Brooke's hands was the same one she'd seen countless times over the years as her Gram cooked. A rush of realization struck, and she lifted the cup toward Mack triumphantly.

She all but shouted the words. "*Christmas cookies.*"

Mack had no idea what she was talking about, but he grinned. "Okay?"

Brooke didn't care that she sounded confused. She turned back to Geraldine and gave her a huge hug. "Thank you, it's wonderful."

The gift-giving continued. In some places around the room, wrapping paper flew as if two-year-olds were involved, but mostly it was the smiles and the laughter that became part of the experience for the next while.

Then Mack offered a significant glance to Geraldine before lifting an oddly shaped package and handing it to Brooke's dad. "Merry Christmas. It's homemade, as per Brooke's instructions. Which means it's a little rough around the edges, but I hope you enjoy it."

Curiosity on his face, Gary hurried to open the package. Absolute shock registered when he lifted a pair of slippers identical to the ones her grandmother had knit so many of over the years. Alternating tan and brown colours, they weren't quite as perfect as Gram's, but they were most definitely slippers and wearable.

Right then and there, her dad slipped off his shoes and put the slippers on. He stood and stomped a few times, his grin widening. Then he moved to Mack's side, hauled him upright, and hugged him hard. "Thank you, son."

Brooke had a perfect view of Mack's face at that moment. The sheer joy reflected there shone as brightly as any star.

It was a couple hours later before they escaped the games and the laughter, and the three of them returned to the apartment over the shop.

The first thing Brooke did was haul out the ingredients to make cookies. "That's why the recipe didn't turn out. We weren't using the right cup."

"Seriously? You're going to bake cookies now?" Mack asked with a laugh.

"If you help so I don't burn them. I'm positive the blue cup is the missing link to our perfect Christmas treats."

Mack shook his head, but he joined her at the counter and began gathering the now-familiar ingredients, only this time they used the magical blue cup to portion out each item.

Once the cookie sheet was safely tucked into the oven, Brooke settled on the couch beside Mack. His arm was curled around her shoulders, and his fingers played in her hair. "I got an update from Brad. I'm on shift starting tomorrow morning for the next four days, but I'll be off after that. We can make plans then, okay?"

She nodded. "You staying with me tonight?"

"Wild horses couldn't tear me away." He nuzzled his nose behind her ear and sent goose bumps rising. "Also, your dad told me he's planning on spending the night out at Ashton's, which means neither of us have to deal with the awkward morning-after at the breakfast table."

"You're going to have to get over that, you realize," she teased.

"Eventually. Maybe once we're actually married."

"Old-fashioned."

"Only a little," he pointed out. "I have no problem being in your bed as much as possible. I just don't want *him* to know that."

She was laughing softly as her dad entered the room and settled in his chair with a contented sigh. He lifted his feet onto the bolster, wiggled his toes, then grinned at Mack. "This is what I wanted. A perfect old-fashioned holiday."

Brooke froze. The scent of spicy cookies was beginning to carry from the kitchen, and they'd managed to do some things from her perfect Christmas list, but so much had been a failure.

"How can you say that?" She directed the question at her father. "There was no turkey dinner, the decorations are over at someone else's house, and we're still waiting for dessert—if it's edible. How is this a perfect old-fashioned holiday?"

He snorted. "Those things are all window dressing. I mean, I enjoy them very much, but what makes it perfect is having a family to share it with." Her father looked at Mack, approval in his expression. "You keep taking care of her like you have over this past year, and I know she'll be happy in the future, no matter what."

Mack's arm tightened around her, cradling her close. "I plan on it, sir."

"That's all a man can ask for, son." He glanced at Brooke sheepishly before turning back to Mack. "For most of this past year, I kept catching myself a half second before calling you *son*. Brooke teased that I'd forgotten your name, but it was easier to not call you anything than get my hopes up. I didn't want to scare either of you off being together. It's kind of nice to be able to just relax and say it. To know you're going to be around for good."

Gary opened up his magazine and proceeded to ignore them.

Brooke felt dazed. She twisted far enough to look into Mack's face. He had a pleased-as-punch expression that wasn't going away anytime soon.

That night as they lay in her bed, the apartment quiet, he was still smiling to beat the band.

His smile got bigger when he sat up enough to grab another cookie off the tray on the side table.

"Your Blue Cup cookies are every bit as good as you'd said they'd be," Mack informed her between crunches. "Sweet and spicy and exactly how Christmas should taste. I hid a dozen of them before your Dad loaded up a bag to take to Ashton's."

"Dad packed the slippers you made and took them along as well." She trailed her fingers over Mack's chest, stroking the soft skin over firm muscle. "I think you'll have to take up knitting in your spare time, just to keep him supplied."

"It'll be worth it," Mack promised. "Have to confess it kinda chokes me up every time he calls me *son*."

It did the same to her. "You're good to him. And you're fantastic to me. Thank you for the picture."

She glanced at the dresser beside her bed where she'd placed the framed shot of the two of them. It was a selfie taken on a day hike up into the mountains. They'd been goofing off and taking silly pictures, but then she'd wanted a serious couple shot. He'd clicked a few with them both supposedly looking at his phone.

The picture he'd blown up had caught a moment when she was staring straight at the camera, the wilderness all around them, and Mack—

All his focus was on her. And while on that long-ago day he hadn't yet said the words, his expression clearly said what was in his heart.

"I love you." The deep rumble of his voice pulled her back to face him.

"I love you too. Obviously, since I'm letting you eat cookies in my bed."

Mack laughed as he caught her hand. He pressed a kiss to her palm, then a second kiss to where his ring sat. Brooke eased back beside him, accepting his embrace and his caresses, luxuriating in his complete attention as he brought them together again.

As they finished with limbs tangled and bodies sated, she laid her head on his chest and sighed.

"I guess there's nothing more old-fashioned about Christmas than love."

Mack stroked his fingers through her hair and rumbled his agreement. "It's everything I ever wished for."

EPILOGUE

Early December, one year later...

There was no reason Ryan Zhao had to go that night other than restlessness had returned with a vengeance, turning his thoughts into a whirl of anger and grief. Sleep was out of the question, and with Talia happily enjoying a sleepover with her friends, he didn't need to stay home.

As usual, his wanderings led him to the cemetery outside Heart Falls. His wife wasn't buried there, but in another silent, cold place far away. Yet the familiar feeling of the place of remembrance was enough to link the spots in his heart. He couldn't visit Justina's resting spot, but she was still somehow *there.*

And the lights were here. The little lights in the trees and hanging from miniature shepherd hooks, all of them scattered around the setting to add an element of fantasy to the otherwise practical and solemn environment. They were solar-powered, and there'd been so little snow that winter season that all the black-topped panels were exposed to the short daylight sunshine. Batteries charged, the lights burned brightly, although they wouldn't last all night the way they did in the summer.

Ryan paced the perimeter of the graveyard, his boots scuffling the scant inch of snow on the tough prairie grass outside the black wrought-iron fence. He picked up the occasional bit of garbage that had been carried in on the wind and caught on the metal railings, tucking the scraps in his pocket.

Like most, this graveyard was a mix of old and new. Tall markers held older dates, with faded flowers in the holders by the black granite rising from the thin layer of white. In the third row over where someone from the community had been buried recently, the mound of dirt over the grave rose higher than the pathways and grass around it.

Solemn. Waiting.

Restful, which made Ryan take a deep breath and let it out slowly.

"I miss you, sweet one," he confessed. "So much. But it feels as if..."

The wind, the ever-present and seemingly determined wind, gusted at that moment. It lifted his hair as if ghostly fingers had run through it in a caress. Icy cold yet refreshing, his cheeks felt kissed by winter's touch.

It feels as if I'm ready to love again.

Ryan hadn't expected the confession to come so clearly, not even to himself. But it was true. Or maybe it wasn't love he was ready for, but Justina had been gone for eight years. He missed her laughter, and her arguments. Missed hearing her talk about the things she'd worked so hard on because they'd been important to her.

He missed company. *Adult* company, and no number of boys' nights out or gatherings with friends, Talia in tow, could meet those needs.

He wanted a partner to talk with about day-to-day plans. To

sit with in front of a fire while they read. A woman he could hold during the night. And yes, if he was having a mental confess-all party, he wanted someone to enjoy physical pleasures with again.

"It's time," he told Justina, offering the words to the sky. "It seems wrong, and yet it feels exactly right."

Another gust of wind.

He laughed, lifting his collar then replacing one of the glittering lights that had tipped onto its side. "Meeting someone here in Heart Falls is going to be tough, though. I might have to ask for help. But God forbid I mention this to my parents. They'll be matchmaking before I finish saying 'I plan to start dating again.'"

The temperature continued to drop, and Ryan moved slowly back to his truck. He was glad his wandering feet had brought him out. It had felt right to be there. To actually say the words that had been in his heart for the last months.

It was time to live that part of his life again.

The engine coughed once then turned over, and he made a mental note to make an appointment for Brooke to check it as soon as possible.

His friends—maybe it was seeing them so in love that had finally made Ryan realize he needed more. Now, nearly a year after he'd teased Mack about it being time to get his act together, it was clear Brooke and Mack were a forever thing.

Before Mack could start poking about when *Ryan* was going to get a move on, he would.

The turnoff from the cemetery to the secondary highway was ice-slick, and even with winter tires, Ryan had to work to keep on the road. He slowed, cautiously following the curving road around Heart Falls to the small house he owned on the semirural outskirts.

Light snow had begun to fall, the flakes creating a blinding curtain across the road. Ryan adjusted the high beams to better cut through the strange glowing—

A light flashed to his left where there should be no light.

Ryan checked in his rearview mirror to make sure there was no one on his tail, then he slowed completely, pulling over far enough to the side of the road so his truck was safe. He glanced back over his shoulder, but nothing seemed out of place. No lights. Nothing wrong.

It would be easy to carry on. To engage the engine and head home to where warmth waited. But his gut wouldn't allow it. The same knot of tension that had struck so many years ago when Justina had casually mentioned she had a headache...

A premonition? Something on the wind calling for his attention? Ryan didn't consider himself superstitious, but he believed there were things that couldn't be explained.

He turned on his hazard lights and pulled his emergency flashlight from under the seat.

The wind jerked his door from his fingers, and snow slammed into him like rocks. Determinedly, he paced back toward the spot where he'd seen something, the glowing circle from the flashlight bouncing over the ground to allow him to pick steady footing.

A low hum cut through the wind, and Ryan frowned as he hurried forward, the road still dark and empty. It seemed he was the only one foolish enough to use this relatively remote section of highway this late on such a wintery night.

He crossed the road, adrenaline pounding through his system.

Or not the *only* one foolish enough to be out driving—because tire tracks lay before him, disappearing down the embankment toward the river. The faintest glow of red was visible between snowy whirls, then the sound of an engine choked to a stop and the lights grew dimmer.

Ryan stepped off the embankment and rushed to help.

New York Times Bestselling Author Vivian Arend invites you to Heart Falls. Most people who call it home have lived for here for generations, or they're looking for a new start and a break from old routines.

Heart Falls is the perfect place for love to come calling and send everyone whirling in its wake.

Each of these titles is a stand alone, feel-good, "Hallmark with heat" written with love for those who cherish a chance to escape into a happily-ever-after during the holiday season.

Holidays at Heart Falls
A Firefighter's Christmas Gift
A Soldier's Christmas Wish
A Hero's Christmas Hope
A Cowboy's Christmas List
A Rancher's Christmas Kiss

The Stones of Heart Falls
A Rancher's Heart
A Rancher's Song
A Rancher's Bride
A Rancher's Love
A Rancher's Vow

ABOUT THE AUTHOR

New York Times and *USA Today* bestselling author Vivian Arend loves to share the products of her over-active imagination with her readers. She writes contemporary, western, and light-hearted paranormal romances. The stories are humorous yet emotional, usually with a large cast of family or friends, and a guaranteed happily-ever-after. Vivian lives in British Columbia, Canada, with her husband of many years—her inspiration for every hero and a willing companion for all sorts of adventures.

www.vivianarend.com